My Ex-Best Friend

A Novel By
D. G. Curry

ISBN: 0989526909
ISBN-13: 978-0-9895269-0-6

DEDICATION

To our young readers. Think first. Act second. And be
amazing in all that you do!

JACKSON HOME – FIRST DAY OF SCHOOL

"I said I'm up!" Shouts 13 year-old Monica Jackson. Her voice reflects the impatience of an oh-so-grown teenager. She flips wild strands of glossy black hair out of her eyes as she sits hunched over on her plush pink twin-size bed. Waiting for her mother's response, Monica rubs the sleep from her eyes. But thankfully, her mom doesn't reply. So of course, Monica takes this as her cue to crawl back under the covers for a few more minutes of peace. After all, it's the first day of school; she has the rest of the school year to get up on time.

Monica's auburn eyes disappear behind the shade of her eyelids. Her lengthy eyelashes flutter as she searches for the sweet sleep spot that overtakes her just before her dreams. But as Monica is drifting back to sleep, her ears catch the sound of her creaking bedroom door. Only one person in this house would dare open her bedroom door without knocking.

"G.G.! Get out of my room!" Monica screams. She leaps out of bed wearing only an oversized Winnie the Pooh t-shirt, and hurls her pillow across the room. But she misses her target as G.G. dodges the pillow. Undaunted and dressed in an increasingly wrinkled polo shirt and khaki shorts, 8 year-old menace, Gilbert Gregory is just too swift for his big sister.

This isn't exactly the first time that G.G. has harassed his sister. Since he was able to crawl, G.G. has made it his mission in life to annoy Monica by any means necessary. When he was only three years old, he cut the heads off all of her teddy bears and by the time he was five, he had given her favorite coat to a homeless person and fed her homework to a stray dog.

Now, crouched on the floor in attack mode, inhaling the scent of the recently vacuumed shag carpet, G.G. curls his lips and sets his sights on Monica as he squeezes the trigger of his deluxe edition Super Soaker. Monica dashes around the room trying to dodge the stream of water. Meanwhile, everything in sight, including posters, stuffed animals and two shopping bags filled with new school clothes are all doused with water.

G.G. rolls around on the floor cackling uncontrollably when he notices that his Super Soaker's water tank has emptied. Realizing that the fun is over, the wide-eyed terror hops up and darts out of the room slamming the door behind him before Monica can give chase.

The morning sunlight trickles into the room through the mini-blinds, bouncing from the blue walls to the pink carpet, highlighting the water damage caused by little G.G.

It dawns on Monica that she may be able to use this sneak attack as an excuse to get her room repainted. The color scheme for the room has been blue and pink since before Monica was born. Her parents weren't sure if they were having a boy or a girl, so Monica's dad thought that he'd play it safe by using both colors.

But as Monica stands there plotting the best way to get a total room makeover, a cold chill whips down her spine causing her to turn around and survey the rest of the damage. It's at this moment that Monica rests her eyes on a shopping bag full of clothes. A steady stream of water leaks from the corner of the bag into a growing puddle below.

"I am going to k…"

She doesn't even get the words out of her mouth before she glances at her clock. "7:30?" She shrieks. "I'm gonna be late!" With no time to dry her new clothes, Monica scrambles to find an outfit in her cramped closet.

Fortunately, like most teenagers, Monica has perfected the art of speed dressing and she sprints downstairs within 10 minutes. It's a new personal record. And it is just enough time to catch her family finishing breakfast.

Mrs. Ann Jackson, who is dressed in her teal nursing scrubs reaches in the cabinet and pulls a strawberry Pop Tart out of the box. Monica's mother is the type of no nonsense mom who was probably a drill sergeant in another life. As healthy and fit as the day she left college, Mrs. Jackson is a no muss, no fuss kind of woman. Her thick black shoulder-length hair is pulled tight into a bun, and her face is void of all make up as usual.

"Here's your breakfast." Mrs. Jackson says handing the pastry to Monica. "Mom, a Pop Tart? What about eggs and bacon?" Monica complains. "Eggs and bacon are for people that get dressed on time, young lady." Scolds her father, Jerome Jackson.

He's not exactly father knows best – more like father tries his best. But no matter how flustered Mr. Jackson may get when dealing with his daughter's issues, he's a good provider. And most of the time, Monica is proud to call him dad.

Mr. Jackson takes a sip of orange juice. He straightens his tie. Then, as is his habit, he slicks the top of his head. It really doesn't make sense because he keeps his haircut so short you'd have to look twice to realize he even has hair. Monica's mom says that men on Mr. Jackson's side of the family tend to bald early. So Monica's dad is just taking a necessary precaution.

Mr. Jackson returns to reading the morning paper as Monica protests. "But it's not my fault. It was G.G." She says pointing at her little brother. "I was getting out of bed when he…"

"Monica!" Interrupts her mother. "Why aren't you wearing your new school clothes? Why did we just spend all that money on clothes if you're still going to where your old things?"

Not actually wanting to hear an answer, Mrs. Jackson just rolls her eyes and starts digging through her purse before handing Monica a five-dollar bill. "This is for lunch." Mrs. Jackson says. "Please try to eat something healthy."

"Don't you even want to know why I'm late?" Monica asks. "No." Her mother says. "I want you to know why you're late so that you can make sure it doesn't happen again." Mrs. Jackson answers in truly annoying parent rhetoric.

"Gilbert Gregory, come get your lunch before you two miss the bus." Mrs. Jackson says holding out a brown bag lunch for her boy genius. G.G. hops up from his seat at the table and tackles the lunch bag.

"Miss the bus?" Squeals Grandma Jackson, the family matriarch. She laughs gently. Her high-pitched voice springs from the family room.

Monica can remember a lot of family discussions a few years ago that led to the decision to have granny Jackson come live with the family. And not one of those discussions mentioned the wigs that look like dead squirrels, the faint old person smell, or the endless re-runs of *Murder She Wrote*.

"They both already missed the bus. I saw the buses drive by a while ago." Grandma says, shuffling in into the kitchen, trying not to trip on her blue terrycloth housecoat. "Granny, why didn't you say anything?" G.G. asks. "I'm sorry, child." Grandma says. "But I don't get paid to watch out for your bus." Huffs Grandma as she plops down at the kitchen table and snags a banana from the fruit bowl.

"Whatever." Mrs. Jackson says to no one in particular, though clearly annoyed with everyone. "Kids, get your backpacks and let's go, now." Barks Mrs. Jackson. In a whirlwind of books, bags and goodbye kisses, she leads Monica and G.G. out of the house.

Just 5 minutes later and the Jackson family's green Ford Fusion approaches C. Edwards Middle School, one of two middle schools located in the town of Brooksville. The car zips down the tree-lined streets as birds chirp and the smell of fresh cut grass completes the middle-American scene on this brisk September morning.

An intense queasiness washes over Monica as she recalls the horror that awaits her at school. She has dreaded this day the entire summer and now Monica is just moments away from re-living the worst day of her life. And to make things worse, she's going to be seen with her mom and her horrible little brother.

All of a sudden, Monica jumps up from her slouched position in the back seat. She scans the neighborhood and shouts "Mom! Can you stop here?"

"For what?" Mrs. Jackson questions. "We're still more than two blocks away from school."

"Please mom." Monica begs. "Just pull over here."

"Please mom." G.G. mimics. The little monster chuckles from the front passenger seat. "She doesn't want to be seen with us, mom." G.G. says, exposing his sister's greatest fear. "Shut up Gilbert!" Monica snaps.

"Is that what this is about, Monica?" her mother asks. "No." Monica says, lying. "I just want to walk."

Mrs. Jackson scoffs at Monica's excuse. She tells her daughter "Don't be silly. When I was your age, I used to love to be seen with my mother."

Now who's lying?

But it doesn't matter. The family Fusion pulls into the semicircle in front of C. Edwards Middle School despite Monica's protest. She peers out of the window. Kids and administrators swarm around the school courtyard, riding that first-day-of-school buzz.

Monica gazes at the school. The massive brick building seems smaller than she remembers. It seems more confined.

Monica can't help but feel a little sick as she slinks out of the car. Her stomach is churning faster and faster. But it's time for her to face the music.

"We love you, honey." Says Mrs. Jackson as she waves goodbye while the Fusion pulls away from the curb. Monica watches them drive off before she finally turns to face the eighth grade.

The sun cascades over the school grounds as Monica stands at the main entrance of C. Edwards Middle School, clutching her cherry Jansport backpack. Throngs of seventh and eighth graders pour into the mouth of the building. But Monica stands frozen, wondering for the first time this morning if anyone will notice that her outfit is last season Gap and not this season Forever 21.

But the thought quickly passes when Monica remembers that there are much bigger issues that she will have to deal with this year than explaining why she didn't wear her new clothes on the first day of school. Around here C. Edwards isn't just a middle school. For seventh and eighth graders on the north side of Brooksville, C. Edwards is life. And the tiny voice in the back of Monica's mind keeps reminding her that it was only a few months ago, that her life changed forever.

C. EDWARDS MIDDLE SCHOOL - MORNING

The familiar sights and sounds of the school send memories of last year's humiliation rushing through Monica's mind. Pushing back the wave of emotion, she takes a deep breath and begins making her way through the crowded main entrance. Once inside, Monica makes a beeline for the math corridor, otherwise known as the eighth grade hallway because the majority of the eighth graders' lockers are located there.

Examining her class schedule for the first time since it arrived in the mail, Monica reads the locker number and immediately locates her locker halfway down the hall. She fiddles with the combination until the locker pops open on the third attempt. To Monica's surprise, no one seems to be staring or laughing at her, yet. She thought for sure that at least one person would shout something rude to her by the time she reached her locker.

Of course, the only thing that worries Monica more than the nosy masses, is running into Jenna Arnold.

In the world of adolescent girls, friends become enemies and enemies become friends on almost a daily basis. But ever so often, there comes an absolute best friend, who through a series of unthinkable events becomes an archenemy. That girl is Jenna.

Throughout the hallway, squeals abound as friends' reunite, excited to embark upon their last year of middle school. Near the entrance of the eighth grade hallway the jocks gather in their usual spot, just steps away from the cheerleaders. First period hasn't even started, yet all of the cliques are already in place.

Monica jams her notebooks into her locker and slams the door shut just as Tammy Olsen approaches. Tammy has always been the sort of girl that is going to be absolutely stunning. But she's the only one who can't see it. Even at the age of thirteen, her honey-toned skin is flawless.

Her mother is African American and her dad is Samoan, but Tammy describes herself as a rainbow because of her mixed heritage.

One of Monica's closest friends since the third grade, Tammy's warm smile is a welcome relief to our stressed-out heroine. "Hey Tam!" Monica exclaims, unable to conceal her excitement as Tammy walks over.

Tammy's shimmering black locks are pulled back in a ponytail and her arms are folded in front of her with three notepads perched tightly in her grip. "Hey Mon." Responds Tammy, much less enthused.

Monica slings her backpack over her shoulder and prepares to greet her friend with a hug but Tammy shies away, still clutching her notepads. "What's your problem?" Monica says, a bit put off by Tammy's cold reception.

"Oh nothing." Tammy tries to assure her. "I'm just a little tired. You know, first day of school and everything. But hey, it's good to see you."

Tammy brushes past her friend, but Monica isn't one to be blown off so easily. She knows what it's like to lose a good friend and Tammy is just about the only good friend Monica has left. "Hey!" She says, grabbing Tammy by the arm. "Is this how you treat someone you haven't seen in two months?"

"No, you don't understand." Tammy says, defending her actions. "I don't understand what?" Monica responds. "I understand that on the last day of school I lost one best friend and now on the first day of this school year it looks like I'm losing the other one."

This was the first summer in years that Monica and her two best friends didn't spend the entire summer hanging out at the in-door pool at the community center or watching the boys from school play basketball at the park. For years, the girls were inseparable. But middle school has a way of changing people, and Monica has good reason to worry about her friendship with Tammy.

"Monica, just shut up, for a minute, OK?" Tammy leans close to Monica and whispers. "I have to show you something." She says, still clinging to her notepads. "Come on."

Tammy drags her friend to the girls' bathroom. Monica sets her belongings on the sink and scrunches her face in confusion as Tammy looks under the shabby stall doors to make sure no one else is in the bathroom. Already tiring of Tammy's odd behavior, Monica's eyes dart from her own reflection in the dull mirrors to the tasteless yellow tiles adorning the bathroom walls before refocusing on Tammy.

"What's going on, Tam? You're starting to freak me out, and the first bell's going to ring in any minute." Monica says as if she's really worried about being late to class.

Tammy takes a deep breath. "Mon, something happened to me this summer and I'm still not really sure how to deal with it."

"Is it your parents? Did they get a divorce?" Monica asks. "Your dad was cheating, wasn't he? I knew it! I can spot a cheater a mile away."

"What? No!" Tammy gasps. "It's got nothing to do with my parents."

Tammy fidgets a few seconds more. Then at last, after another deep breath, Tammy lowers the notepads she's been holding in front of her and says, "I got these."

"Get out!" Monica exclaims, as she stares bug-eyed at Tammy's fully developed chest. Tammy studies Monica's face, trying to make sense of her reaction. She then turns her attention to her own reflection and her "friends" that she's unable to hide beneath a fitted Lacoste polo that's tucked into a coffee-colored skirt.

"Where did those come from?" Monica says, still staring.

"I don't know." Tammy responds. "It's like one month I had to get rid of my training bra and by the end of the summer, I went up three bra sizes."

Monica, still speechless, continues to stare at her newly endowed friend, before her eyes drift down to her own chest. "Wow." She mumbles. "That's amazing. Do you know how I can get a pair?" Both girls force a smile.

But Monica is still stunned. Is this really Tammy, the same girl who cried all night the first time her mom let her spend the night at the Jackson's home when the girls were five? Tammy's beauty was always understated and simple, not va-va-va-voom!

Tammy takes Monica by the hand. "Something else happened too." She says. Monica gawks at her best friend, preparing herself for more astounding news. "I got my period." Tammy says, bursting with excitement.

Staring blankly at Tammy, Monica is speechless for the first time in her life. "Mon?" Tammy says, waving her hand in front of Monica's face. "Are you ok?"

Since the beginning of sixth grade Monica has been expecting a visit from the feminine fairy. She always thought of herself as being more mature than most girls in her grade, so at the time, it only seemed natural that she would be one of the first girls to get her period. But that was two years ago and Monica is privately panicking about the fact that it hasn't happened yet.

"Huh? Oh yeah, I'm fine." Monica replies, coming back to reality. "I'm just, I'm just so happy for you. You know, for a while I thought you were going to actually be an eighth grader who hasn't had her period."

"So you got yours too?"

Tammy's question might as well be a swift punch in the gut. "Of course I got my period." Monica lies. "I mean, who hasn't, right?"

"Oh my God. Wasn't it the worst?" Tammy says laughing. "Wasn't what the worst?" Monica asks curiously. "Getting your first period, genius. I got mine the week we went on vacation. I was literally, in line at Six Flags when it happened. It was so gross." Tammy says, reminiscing. "What about you? When'd you get yours?"

Monica flips through a mental Rolodex of fibs. She is about to spin a brilliant web of lies to her best friend when suddenly the "warning" bell rings.

"Oh great." Tammy mutters. "It's funny, I got so caught up that I almost forgot we were at school. Hey, maybe you can tell me your horror story after class, today." Tammy says with a smile. "Sure." Monica says. "You won't believe what happened."

Monica and Tammy gather their things and begin to head out of the girls' bathroom when Tammy stops Monica in her tracks. "Listen, Mon. Thanks for being such a good friend. I was really uncomfortable about the whole big boob thing. So thanks for not making me feel like a freak."

The duo emerges from the bathroom and walks down the Foreign Languages corridor to their first period classes. They stop every few feet to exchange summer stories and examine class schedules with a few faux friends as they slowly make their way to class. While the girls are walking, Monica becomes increasingly aware of a large number of male admirers that are gazing in the girls' direction. She takes one look at Tammy – who is no longer concealing her weapons – and Monica is positive that she knows exactly what the boys are staring at. After all, they are boys. And everyone knows that boys are only good for two things, playing sports and gawking at cute girls. And Tammy is officially a "cute" girl.

But as the girls navigate their way down the hallway, Monica notices something. Kids are slowly beginning to look at her. Except, they aren't just looking at her. They are staring and whispering. Monica's apprehension grows as she feels more and more piercing glares with each step she takes. But suddenly, all of the chatting and staring comes to a screeching halt.

Monica looks over her shoulder just in time to catch the sea of middle school kids parting to either side of the hallway to make room for…The Dolls. Monica can almost hear the evil theme music as the four girls strut towards her.

Rumor has it that The Dolls are the most popular girls to ever walk through the doors of C. Edwards Middle School. They are part cheerleader, part preppie, part honor roll students and ALL evil. They are Shannon, Erica, Lauren...and Jenna.

No one really knows when the tradition started, but long ago when people watched videos tapes instead of digital streaming and people listened to cassettes instead of iTunes, four of the school's most popular eighth grade girls founded Brooksville's first and only junior sorority. The sisters of <u>D</u>elta <u>O</u>mega <u>L</u>ambda <u>S</u>orority were practically nicknamed The Dolls overnight. They used their "sisterhood" to become the most popular and envied group of girls at school. By the middle of that school year every girl in the school wanted to be a Doll. So about a month before the girls graduated to high school, they decided to handpick four seventh grade girls that would become the next year's Dolls.

Since then, the tradition has continued and each year the seventh grade girls at C. Edwards spend the last two months of the school year primping and preening, holding on to the slim hope of being selected to become a sister of Delta Omega Lambda Sorority.

Every preteen girl in Brooksville wants to be a Doll. One year a girl actually transferred from another middle school just so that she could be considered. Of course she wasn't chosen. The Dolls would never pick someone so desperate for attention.

This year's Dolls are the most fierce, feared, and smart girls to ever grace the halls of C. Edwards Middle School. And today they have their sights set on Monica Jackson.

Monica's grip on her backpack tightens as she considers running away. But it's too late. The moment of truth has arrived. Jenna and Monica lock eyes. It's the first time they've been face-to-face since last school year.

Jenna Arnold, The Dolls unquestioned leader, has somehow managed to assume control of the school despite spending half of the summer vacationing with her family in Spain. She is Barbie with B Cups. From her Prada handbag to her plastic smile.

Monica tries her best to maintain her tough facade as she stares down her mortal enemy. However, this isn't an easy feat considering how well Jenna knows Monica. The whole school is well aware of the fact that Jenna isn't just one of The Dolls. She's Monica's ex-best friend.

"Hello M.J." Jenna says with a smirk. She's the only person who has ever referred to Monica by her initials and lived to tell the story. Monica always felt like M.J. was a nickname for boys, but she let her best friend slide. Too bad Jenna isn't her best friend anymore.

"Let me think." Jenna continues. "When was the last time we saw each other?"

Monica takes a long, deliberate breath. Her mind fills with thoughts of the detention and suspension to come if she acts on her impulse to strangle Jenna. But she is able to compose herself and says, "I think you know when we saw each other last. It was around the same time you sold your soul."

"Geez, MJ. You're so dramatic." Jenna replies, her Mac lip-gloss glistening on her lips. "Was I being dramatic when you stabbed me in the back?" Monica barks. The crowd is stunned.

"Oh get over yourself, MJ" Jenna fires back. "Whether it was me, or somebody else, eventually you were going to be put in your place. At the bottom." Jenna beams triumphantly as she watches Monica's expression shrink from fearless to fearful in less than a second.

"You're pathetic!" Monica blurts out with nothing left to say. The Dolls burst into laughter as if sharing an inside joke.

"I'm pathetic?" Jenna says, returning her attention to Monica. "Your outfit is pathetic. What is that, the Salvation Army fall collection?" Jenna laughs as the three hyenas join her in mocking her former friend.

"Hey guys!" Tammy interrupts. "We shouldn't argue."

"Tam?" Jenna says surprised, as if it's been two years and not two months since she's seen Tammy. "Wow, you look really hot." Jenna says.

Tammy can't help but feel validated; even if she does have her own baggage from her own lost friendship with Jenna.

"Well, well. Someone got a visit from the fem fairy." Remarks Lauren Swarth, a petite firecracker.

"I'll say." Jenna replies. "It looks like our little Tammy is a big girl now." Jenna says, discretely sizing Tammy up.

"Don't act like you care about Tammy or anyone else." Monica says.

"You again?" Jenna says exasperated as if she thought Monica had vanished into thin air. Jenna extends her hand and right on cue, the ultra fit Shannon slips her cabana bag from her shoulder. "Here." Jenna says as she rips a copy of "In Style Magazine" from Shannon's bag.

Jenna shoves the magazine into Monica's chest. "Read this and take notes. Then see if you can put together a decent outfit." Jenna stomps away with Lauren and Erica close on her heals.

"Um, can you bring that back to me when you're done? I haven't finished reading it." Shannon says to Monica before running off to catch up with her friends.

Emotionally overwhelmed, Monica fights back tears and the urge to smack everyone in sight. Left with no other alternative, she slings her backpack over her shoulder and hurries away. Her eyes bubble as she presses through the horde of snickering on-lookers.

SOCIAL SCIENCE CLASS – AFTERNOON

At long last, the first period bell finally rings and the official start of the school year arrives. The rest of the day drags for Monica as she fumes over her run-in with Jenna.

Thoughts of revenge flood Monica's mind. She can't seem to focus on anything else during the remainder of her classes. At least that is the case until seventh period advanced social sciences class.

How did I get this class anyway? Monica wonders. Rarely does Monica perform above her C+ average. And she's never shown an aptitude for any kind of science, social or otherwise. So landing a spot in an advanced class is beyond weird.

Mr. Braybrand – old enough to be a teacher, young enough to still look kind of cool – leans against his desk taking attendance. He's a tall man. He was probably a star baseball player in a high school somewhere about 10 years ago.

Mr. Braybrand continues reading the roll, periodically brushing back his wavy brown hair. He's done that four times by Monica's count. She was forced to take a seat at the very front of the classroom. That's what happens when you walk in the door just before the bell rings. The rest of the kids were already situated when Monica arrived and now the only empty seat in the entire room is right next to Monica.

By the last period of the day, the novelty of the new school year has already worn off. So Mr. Braybrand's most difficult task will be keeping the kids awake. "Ok, guys." Mr. Braybrand says. "That's just about everybody. It looks like we've got a pretty full class. My name is Mr. Braybrand. But you kids can call me, Mr. B."

Mr. B swings around his desk and starts writing his name on the chalkboard. "The one thing that you should know about my class is that I don't give a lot of tests." The students respond with cheers and shouts. "I do, however, give a number of pop quizzes." Mr. B continues.

The cheers give way to a chorus of boos. "All right guys, settle down." Mr. B says, picking up a textbook. "Today we'll have an overview of the course and tomorrow I'll provide a few details on the work that will be expected of you."

Monica attempts to stifle a deep yawn as she resists the urge to fall asleep in class. Fortunately, Mr. B's class zips by and the bell rings, jarring Monica from her haze.

Content not to do any homework on the first day of school, Monica dumps all of her books into her locker and slams it shut. She dodges the slackers, goths, jocks and skaters on her way to the front of the school as she looks for Tammy. A few short moments later, Monica stands near the front office waiting for her friend. But Tammy doesn't show up.

Tired of waiting, Monica ventures out to the front of the building after about five minutes of watching kids file out of the building. All around, students hustle to the remaining school buses. To her left, Monica spots a group of girls hanging out near the Spirit Bench.

The Spirit Bench is the over-sized park bench located in the middle of the school's front lawn. Three times a year, the cheerleaders decorate the bench with paint, posters and pom-poms in support of the school's athletic programs. It's also the unofficial hangout spot of the popular girls.

Maybe that's why Monica can't believe her eyes. Amongst the self-absorbed rich girls and cheerleaders, Tammy is standing, once again covering her chest with a set of notebooks as she musters up an unconvincingly fake laugh.

Confused, Monica marches over to the group. "Tammy?" She calls.

"Oh hey, Mon." Tammy says walking over to her friend. "I was wondering where you were. I've been waiting forever."

"Did you just have a brain fart?" Monica says. "We were supposed to meet in front of the office, just like we always do."

"Oh, right. Hey, my bad." Tammy replies. "Oh well, no biggie."

No biggie? Monica says to herself. She tries to play it cool despite not knowing exactly how to react to Tammy's carefree attitude. After all, it is a "biggie." Last year, they met every single day after school in the same exact spot and suddenly Tammy doesn't remember?

Tammy doesn't give Monica much time to dwell on the issue though as she heads towards the buses. "Bye Tammy!" Shout the picturesque pep squad girls who remain huddled around the Spirit Bench. Monica rushes to catch up with Tammy who hardly seems to notice that Monica is tagging along.

"Since when do you hang out at the Spirit Bench?" Monica asks. "I don't know." Tammy says. "I was just talking to some of the girls in class and we ended up walking over there. What gives, anyway?"

"Oh, it's nothing." Monica says as the two of them walk down the block from the school. "I was just standing inside waiting for you. I missed the bus because I thought you were still inside, somewhere."

"I'm sorry. I forgot." Tammy says nonchalantly.

"Hmm," Monica sighs. "What?" Tammy questions a bit defensively. "Oh it's nothing. I guess I should have known that you wouldn't be in our normal spot. I mean, this morning you didn't exactly have my back when Jenna and her little trolls we're embarrassing me in front of the whole school."

"What did you want me to do, Monica?" Tammy pleads. "You're the one who was egging them on."

Monica clears her throat, planning to defend herself when out of nowhere a car horn interrupts the girls' conversation. Beep, beep. The girls swivel their heads to see the Jackson family's familiar green Fusion pull up beside them.

The window glides down and Mrs. Jackson says "Hey honey. Hi Tammy. I was just in the neighborhood and I thought I'd see if you girls caught the bus and what-do-ya-know? You're walking home. Talk about lucky, huh?"

Monica smirks. "Yep. Real lucky."

"Hop in." Mrs. Jackson unlocks the car doors. The girls chuck their backpacks into the car. Monica hops in the front seat and Tammy drops herself into the back seat.

Ring! The first period bell echoes throughout the school and just like a bad dream, Monica looks up to find herself right back in the classroom. She stares at the back of some kid's head while aimlessly strolling through the apps on her phone, hoping something will be intriguing enough to grab her attention.

"Hola. Me llamo Senora Ordonez." The Spanish teacher says, greeting the groggy first period class. "Como estas?" She asks the class for the second day in a row.

"If she is going to ask us the same three questions everyday for the rest of the year, I think I'm going to throw up, un pocquito." Monica replies, pinching the air. Kids in the chairs around her snicker under their breath.

"Perdon, senorita?" Mrs. Ordonez says to Monica. "Um, sorry Senora. No speako espanolo." Monica jokes, getting even more laughs from the class.

"Well maybe you'll understand this," Mrs. Ordonez clarifies in perfect English. If you continue to disrupt my class, you'll be free to leave and come back for after school detention." She says, gesturing towards the door.

Monica slumps back in her chair, but her eyes follow Mrs. Ordonez's finger right out the door. To her surprise, she catches a glimpse of Tammy walking down the hall with Erica Stevens!

Monica spends the rest of first period ignoring Senora Ordonez as she conjugates verbs while Monica's mind runs rampant trying to figure out why Tammy would be hanging out with one of The Dolls. Monica generates excuse after excuse, while trying to keep her mind from considering the possibility that Tammy and Erica may actually be friends.

By the time seventh period arrives, Monica is a wreck. As if catching Tammy giggling with the enemy isn't enough to upset Monica, she doesn't see Tammy during fourth period lunch and her multiple text messages have gone unanswered.

Monica slumps into her seat in Mr. Braybrand's class. Once again, she sit's in the front row. She gazes to her right at the chair next to her. A cold, sinking feeling bottoms out in the pit of her stomach as the empty seat reminds her of own loneliness.

Mr. B walks into class just as the bell rings. He drops his briefcase on his desk and scans the room. "The person sitting next to you will be your study partner for the duration of this semester." He begins. "So I hope you didn't just grab a seat next to your closest friend. Because if he or she doesn't know what they're doing, that is your problem too."

Moans rustle through the classroom from the back of the room all the way to the very front, where Monica glares at the empty seat to her left.

So who is gonna be my partner? Monica thinks to herself. She starts to ponder what it will be like to be the only person in the class without a study partner. Even worse, she wonders what will happen if she is forced to be a third wheel with another group. But that's when it happens. In an instant, the entire school year changes.

The classroom door bursts open and in strolls Johnny Hammond. Every school has a Johnny Hammond. He is the cutest, most popular, most athletic boy in school.

Johnny stands in the doorway looking perfect as usual. His fresh haircut is flawless and there is even a hint of a mustache coming in on his smooth cocoa-colored face.

"Mr. Hammond." Says Mr. B who doubles as the basketball coach. "It's nice of you to join us. I take it that since you are late to my class, you won't mind being early to practice so that you can run a few laps. Take a seat right here." Mr. B says, pointing next to Monica. Johnny sits down and pulls off his backpack, exposing more muscles through his mesh C. Edwards' football t-shirt than any 13-year-old boy should possess.

"Mr. Hammond, this is your study partner, Monica." Mr. B explains. Johnny flashes Monica with his beautiful smile. She gazes at those perfect teeth and she practically faints when Johnny inadvertently brushes her shoulder as he gets settled in his seat.

Simply gorgeous, she swoons.

As Mr. B continues speaking, Monica fights the repeated urge to look into Johnny's eyes and tell him to runaway with her. She is so flustered just by Johnny's presence that even when she isn't trying to catch a glimpse of him out of the corner of her eye, she's wondering if he's looking at her.

But in the midst of her daydreaming, Monica becomes aware of the sound of girlish snickering. Every single girl in the class must be utterly envious of her. And though Monica loves the idea of spending time with the hottest guy in her grade, she's also a little bit unnerved by the added attention. She isn't sure if it's Johnny or all of the extra eyes focused on her, but her armpits are dripping with sweat.

As if the imaginary sexual tension isn't enough, Monica spends half of the class glancing back over her shoulder because she is convinced that each snicker coming from the back of the class is aimed at her.

By the end of class the pressure of being partnered with the best catch that C. Edwards Middle School has to offer is already too much. Monica doesn't even acknowledge Johnny when he says goodbye to her after the bell rings. Instead, Monica dips her head and rushes out of the room and straight towards her locker.

As she shoves her way through the crowd, a gentle put firm hand takes her by the arm. Monica swings around to find herself falling deep into Johnny's eyes.

"Hi." Johnny says. "I didn't get a chance to introduce myself." He extends his hand towards Monica. "I'm Johnny."

"Hi Johnny. I'm in love. I mean, I'm Monica." She stumbles. "I guess we're going to be parents, I mean, partners." Monica continues to fumble.

"Yep." Johnny agrees. "Can I have your cell number? I'll call you and we can set up some time to study."

Monica peeps at Johnny's cell phone as she whispers her phone number to him. She starts to get a little antsy as she notices a growing number of eyes staring at the couple. But it's too late. They've been spotted.

Lauren Swarth nearly leaps out of her Michael Stars dip-dyed dress when she sets her eyes on the pair of study buddies. "Johnny!" Lauren yelps. "That is it!" She screams as her voice climbs an octave.

Johnny, who is a little too laid back for his own good, is a bit dazed and confused by the scene that Lauren is causing. "Hey Lauren." Johnny says with a smile. "What's going on?"

"What's going on?" Lauren replies. "I'll tell you what's going on, Jonathan Hammond!" Lauren stomps towards her boyfriend. The Dolls form rank behind her.

Stabbing Johnny's chest with her finger, Lauren growls. "Do you think I'm stupid?"

"What? Girl, what are you talking about?"

"I am a Doll!" Lauren bellows.

The gathering group of students can practically feel the anger mounting in Lauren's petite frame. The entire hallway is filled with kids ignoring the fact that they need to catch the bus home.

Monica, on the other hand, would like nothing more than to disappear right now. She wonders if she can sneak away, but she doubts it.

Lauren turns her attention to Monica, pressing her delicate nose within an inch of Monica's face. "I hope you don't really think that my boyfriend would ever dream of hooking up with you." Lauren snarls.

Monica would like to pretend that she doesn't know what Lauren is talking about, but she does. She knows that Johnny and Lauren have been the school's hottest couple since they first kissed at a pool party this summer.

"Lauren, maybe if you actually talked to your boyfriend instead of jumping to conclusions or getting your gossip from US weekly, you'd know that I'm just not interested in your leftovers." Monica snaps.

The crowd erupts! No one can believe that anybody, let alone Monica, would say something so disrespectful to The Dolls.

In C. Edwards Middle School it's a well-known fact that becoming a Doll is like becoming a "made man" in the mafia. Once you reach that status, you're pretty much untouchable.

For once, Lauren is speechless. She can't do anything but scowl and tuck her amber locks behind her ear in an effort to deflect embarrassment. Shannon and Erica try to stifle their giggles as Jenna smirks wickedly.

Lauren paces in front of Johnny like a lion preparing to devour a meal. Not even Johnny knows what to expect. He just stands there, dumbfounded.

"You better listen up, you big piece of crap!" Says Lauren. "Nobody...nobody tries to play me. You and I are over!" She screams.

"But babe." Johnny says, shocked. "What did I do?"

"You know what you did, and you know who you did it with." Lauren says, locking her gaze onto Monica.

"Now wait a minute." Monica says, preparing to defend herself. "Lauren, you can't seriously think that we are dating."

"Just shut up, MJ." Jenna chimes in. A collective gasp overcomes the audience of adolescents. Jenna slides off her sunglasses and shakes her head in disgust. "So what's wrong, MJ? Are you still so upset about Mike Tryst that you had to steal Lauren's boy toy?"

"Did you just call me a boy toy?" Johnny asks, confused.

Just hearing the name Mike Tryst angers Monica. Even though Mike no longer roams the halls of C. Edwards Middle School, his legacy as last year's hottest eighth grader lives on. But despite his legendary sex appeal, Mike Tryst is one person that Monica would like to forget forever.

"I didn't take anyone's boyfriend, Jenna." Says Monica. "I'm not like you."

"Oh God. Here come the waterworks!"

"Bite me!" Monica yells.

"Kiss my…"

"Hey!" A furious Lauren explodes. "Remember me? I'm the one who has a boyfriend standing in the middle of school trying to get another girl's phone number!"

She's back to poking Johnny in his chest. "Johnny, like I said, we're over." Lauren snaps her neck around and heads off in the opposite direction. Her hair whisks as she turns, practically smacking Monica in the face. "Shannon, Erica, let's go!" Lauren barks.

The other Dolls hustle off as Jenna stands with her hand on her hip, still smirking at Monica. "MJ you are so pathetic. This is the eighth grade. It's time for you to grow up and stop being such a sap." Jenna declares before she saunters away.

By now, the crowd is beginning to disperse. Monica chews her bottom lip. Can I get just one day of peace? She wonders.

The weekend couldn't have come soon enough. Monica trudges up the stairs towards her bedroom on Friday afternoon. She pitches her backpack onto her bedroom floor and shuts the door. She doesn't even bother to push her nightgown to the side of her bed as she plops down. Too tired or too lazy to reach over and pick up the television remote control, Monica lies on her bed in silence.

A few minutes later she takes hold of her raggedy teddy bear, Mr. Fluff-n-Stuff, and gazes into his brown button eyes. Monica lounges on her bed, making a mental list of all her social problems. But oddly enough, it's not Jenna or Johnny that she can't stop thinking about. It's Tammy that Monica keeps wondering about. How did she go from being this cute quiet little girl to this Hawaiian Tropics model overnight?

"Why can't I have boobs?" Monica wonders aloud.

All of a sudden Monica hears something. She listens closely. It's the sound of someone laughing!

Fueled with anger, Monica jumps off her bed and storms towards the closet. She flings the door open to find G.G. perched in a pile of dirty clothes. Caught red-handed and no longer able to contain his laughter, G.G. collapses to the floor into a ball of giggling madness. "Boobs!" He screams. "Why can't I have boobs?" G.G. yells, continuing to mock his older sister.

"I hate you!" Monica explodes.

G.G. has been hailed as the family genius ever since he skipped the second grade. So being the smart kid that he is, G.G. senses that it's time to make his exit. He scrambles to his feet and he dives in the direction of the door, but it's too late. Monica pounces on her younger brother and begins wrestling him to the floor, shouting at G.G. as he tries in vain to wriggle away.

The scuffle doesn't go unnoticed however, and soon Monica's bedroom door opens and Grandma Jackson stands in the doorway, hands on her hips. G.G. spots his grandma and yells "Granny, help me!"

"Monica!" Grandma says. "What is going on here? Get off that boy!" Monica pins her brother to the floor. "He was sitting in my closet spying on me, grandma." Returning her focus to back to her beaten brother, Monica proceeds to shake and jab G.G. in his arms as Grandma Jackson looks on.

Mrs. Jackson, already home from an early morning shift at the hospital, hears the commotion and rushes up the stairs to Monica's room. "Monica, what in heaven's name are you doing to your brother? Get off of him right now!" She yells. "But mom." Monica argues. "Now!" Demands her mother.

Monica climbs off her victim, reluctantly loosening her grip on his spider-man T-shirt. Still in shock, Mrs. Jackson turns to Grandma. "Mother Jackson," says Monica and G.G.'s mom. "How can you stand there and let her do that to him?"

"Well it sounded like he needed a good thumping." Grandma Jackson replied. "And she was already doing such a great job, that I didn't feel the need to stop her." Grandma Jackson says before calmly walking away.

Frustrated, Mrs. Jackson takes a deep breath before banishing G.G. to his bedroom. "Go to your room and do your homework, Gilbert." She says pointing down the hallway. "But I did my homework already." G.G. replies. "Well then go do some extra credit." His mother counters. "I did." G.G. says. "I also read the next two chapters in our textbook and I finished an extra page of math problems just for fun."

"Fine." Says an exasperated Mrs. Jackson. "Then just go to your room and act like you're studying! I don't want to hear another peep out of you. Do you understand?" G.G. pokes out his bottom lip and nods his head in agreement as he stumbles to his room.

"Monica." Her mother says. "What was that about?"

"I don't want to talk about it." Monica answers. She walks back over to her bed and lays face down, attempting to find the peace she had before G.G. interrupted. "We're going to talk about this, young lady." Mrs. Jackson says. "But we don't have to do it now." She calmly concludes. "You may not believe me, but I know what it's like to be a teenager." Mrs. Jackson says before closing the door on her way out of the room.

Monica spends the remainder of the afternoon silently cursing her brother's name and thinking thoughts that no sister should have about her baby brother. The afternoon hours drift away into the sunset and Monica stays curled up on her bed, her mind dancing between being asleep and awake.

The sound of light knocking on her bedroom door drags Monica out of her dreary state. Her father pokes his head in the room. "Hi sweetie, I just thought you could use a bite to eat."

He presents her with a plate of pepperoni pizza and a Cherry Coke, her favorite. "Thanks dad." Monica says as she sits up in bed, taking the plate from her dad. Mr. Jackson smiles and begins to walk away before a thought pops into his mind. "Oh, honey, I almost forgot. Your mother and I would like to sit down with you and your brother sometime this weekend to talk. It's nothing big, but we would like to know how everything went in your first week at school." Her dad smiles warmly and closes the door as he exits.

Monica's parents always want to talk to her. Whether it's about school or movies or even boys. But Monica always gives them the same boring responses. And who can blame her? What teenage girl wants to talk to her dad about boys?

No matter, Monica doesn't dwell too long on the idea of discussing her personal life with her folks. Maybe the Cherry Coke made her feel better. Or maybe it's the re-runs of *MADE* on MTV. Regardless of the reason, it isn't long before Monica starts feeling like her normal, sort-of-happy self.

JACKSON HOME – SUNDAY EVENING

The weekend zips by in the blink of an eye. Monica wastes the entire day watching television on Saturday before going to church Sunday morning and suffering through the second half of a Washington Redskins preseason game on Sunday afternoon. Mr. Jackson made it quite clear years ago that Monica will be his sidekick during all NFL games until G.G. is old enough pay attention through all four quarters.

But just as it seems that the weekend is coming to a quick close, Grandma Jackson's voice rings throughout the house. "Jerome!" Grandma Jackson squawks from the comfort of her easy-chair recliner. "Didn't you say that you wanted to talk to these children about school?"

Mr. Jackson, still recovering from his NFL trance says, "Yes, actually I did. Kids, have a seat." G.G. and Monica crouch on the living room floor in front of the couch where Mr. and Mrs. Jackson sit comfortably.

"Now kids." Mrs. Jackson begins. "This is very informal, but your father and I think it's important for us to touch base with you. I mean, you're both growing up so fast and we just want you to know that you can talk to us about anything. Anything." She repeats for emphasis.

Kids who are lucky enough to have parents who actually care about what they're doing should at least listen to what their folks have to say. But do we have to have a family meeting? Monica thinks. All this scene needs is some music and a Bentley and this would turn into an old episode of *Run's House*.

So Monica spends the next fifteen seconds employing the same tactics she uses in school. She sits up straight and avoids eye contact at all costs. Meanwhile, G.G. is on the verge of bursting as he waves his hand in the air trying to get his parents attention. This is one time when Monica would love nothing more than for her overachieving brother to take center stage. Of course, that doesn't happen.

"Monica, let's start with you." Her mother says. "What's on your mind?" Monica freezes. She can't think of even one mundane thing to tell her parents. So after careful thought she gives a classic answer. "Nothing."

"Nothing?" Her father repeats. "Are you sure there isn't anything you'd like to talk about?" Staring at the floor, Monica says "No, not really."

"What about sex?" Grandma Jackson shouts. "Mom, please!" Mr. Jackson gasps. "My little girl is not thinking about sex! She hasn't even had her period yet, for crying out loud!"

"Dad!" Screams an embarrassed Monica. "I can't believe you just said that!"

"Said what? The sex thing?" Monica's dad asks. "You're not really thinking about sex are you?" Mr. Jackson clasps his hands together and looks upward. "Please God, tell me she's not thinking about sex!"

"Of course she's thinking about sex!" Grandma Jackson shouts, nearly tipping out of her chair. "I was thinking about sex when I was young. Although I was much more endowed than she is at her age." Grandma Jackson peeks over at Monica and says again. "Much more endowed."

"Mother Jackson!" Exclaims an appalled Mrs. Jackson as she turns to comfort Monica. "Honey," Her mom says to Monica in her most soothing voice. "We don't have to talk about sex right now, OK?"

"I don't understand why we're talking about sex at all." Shouts a frustrated Mr. Jackson. He stands up and announces. "Nobody is having sex in this house. Not Monica, not me, not your mother, not anyone! Do I make myself clear?"

"Jerome, calm down." Mrs. Jackson interrupts.

G.G., who has had his hand held high in the midst of all the discussion, finally has a moment to speak. "Mommy, I want a period!"

Monica rolls her eyes in disgust, wondering where this conversation went so wrong. "O.K," Mrs. Jackson says firmly to silence the room. "Everyone just take a deep breath and we'll start this over again.

"Gilbert, why don't you tell mom and dad something that's on your mind? Please make sure that it doesn't have anything to do with your sister or her period."

G.G. rocks from side to side rolling his eyeballs around in his head as he hums an unfamiliar tune. Eventually, he stops. His mind settles on one of the many topics popping in and out his busy mind. G.G. hops up and runs into his mother's lap. He giggles and says, "I'm working on a secret mission."

"Oh really?" Mrs. Jackson says, semi-intrigued. "What's this mission about?"

"I can't tell you." G.G. replies. He turns and looks right into Monica's eyes. "It's top secret." He smirks slyly at his big sister. In turn, Monica ignores his taunts by putting her head in her left hand and studying the chipped fingernail polish on her right hand.

She knows better than to worry about what G.G. is up to. When you have a younger brother who is as smart and as strange as Gilbert Gregory Jackson, you tend to experience more than your fair share of science experiment mishaps. Besides, the odd tendencies of an elementary school kid can't trump the issues that Monica is facing at C. Edwards.

She manages to makes it through the rest of the evening without her parents badgering her about deep dark secrets and "confusing feelings." But just as much as Monica wants the family's Sunday conversation to end, she also doesn't want Monday morning to arrive. But time is funny like that. It keeps moving forward whether you want to or not.

After dragging herself out of bed, Monica sprints to the bus stop just in time to catch Bus 13 so that she doesn't have to get chauffeured by her mom again.

Most of the kids getting off Bus 13 are chatting and laughing as they embark on the new school day. Not Monica. She hops off of the bus and briskly makes her way to the seventh grade corridor. From there, Monica walks through a maze of hallways all just to avoid running into The Dolls.

The undercover tactics work and not only does Monica steer clear of The Dolls, but the school day seems to be chugging along just like any other. Monica shirks the urge to nap in Ms. Newsome's history class by doodling in her notebook. She glances up at the clock just as the bell rings, marking the end of third period.

Ms. Newsome, whose hefty frame and stern demeanor have long been her calling cards, shuffles over to the doorway and catches the students before they can leave. "Attention! Attention!" Ms. Newsome bellows. "As you leave, I will be handing out a take-home quiz." A wave of grumbles passes over the classroom as the students pack their belongings and make their way towards the exit.

Monica manages to fiddle around longer than most. As she is packing her notebook Monica senses someone standing over her shoulder. She looks up to see Ebony Ocean hovering over her desk.

Ebony is considered to be a nice person by most accounts. But she does have one huge flaw – she LIVES for juicy rumors.

Monica eyeballs Ebony. She takes note of everything from Ebony's True Religion jeans to her dangling earrings. Ebony smiles cautiously, slightly displaying her glistening braces. "Hi Ebony." Monica says. "Is there something I can help you with?"

"Hi Monica." Ebony begins. "I know all about that embarrassing scene with The Dolls. Well, I just wanted to say that I'm sorry because that's got to really suck."

"Thanks...I think." Monica replies. Hoping that the conversation is over, she begins to head towards the door where Ms. Newsome stands waiting to hand quizzes to the stragglers. "Hey Monica, wait up!" Ebony shouts. "You're going to lunch right? Me too. Do you mind if I walk with you?"

"I guess so." Monica says as she takes a quiz from Ms. Newsome and shoves it into her backpack. The two girls stroll the hallways, from one end of the school to the other until they arrive at the cafeteria. Ebony does most of the talking. But that's typical of Ebony. She rambles on about so many things that Monica can't even keep up until Ebony mentions something very intriguing.

"Oh God! Did you hear that Johnny is going to wait until the end of the week to dump Lauren? You know, it reminds me of the time I was going to cut this girl from the cheer squad. She was the one with the lazy eye that smelled a little funny..."

"Wait! What did you say?" Monica asks, finally catching up to the conversation. "Oh, it was nothing." Ebony recaps. "She just smelled funny. I don't know if it was body odor, or if it was her feet."

"No." Monica shouts. "Did you say that Johnny is going to dump Lauren? I thought she already dumped him."

"Well, duh. Of course she did." Ebony scoffs. "But then she decided to take him back. I mean, come on. He's friggin gorgeous. But he can't keep dating her if he's going to date you." Monica stops in her tracks. "What?" She says in disbelief. "Yeah." Ebony says. "The whole school knows about you two."

Monica's brain melts into a confused pile of mush. Why would people say that I'm dating Johnny? She wonders. Suddenly a few high-pitched shrieks break the momentum of Monica's thoughts. She finds herself in the middle of a small group of hyperactive cheerleaders that consists of Ebony and four friends.

Ebony and the girls try to engage Monica in their conversation filled with the day's new gossip, but Monica needs a minute to herself. Not even a story about Mrs. Hatfield, the gym teacher, bleaching her mustache can keep Monica immersed in the discussion.

Ebony notices Monica slipping away and says "Hey Monica! Same time tomorrow, 'kay?" Monica flashes a fake smile. "Sure." She says, briskly backing away.

Monica scans the cafeteria and decides to grab her food before finding a seat. Spending her lunch money about as wisely as most kids her age, Monica snags a fruit juice and a honey bun out of the vending machines.

"Hey Mon." Tammy says, walking towards Monica carrying her lunch tray. "You'll never guess what happened." Tammy says as she shakes her backpack from her shoulder.

"Hey Tammy." Interrupts Debra, a leggy debutante type. Debra seems to be a nice enough person, as long as you're not poor, or fat or unpopular. Future socialites like her must be very selective of whom they associate with. Which begs the question. Why is she talking to Tammy?

"Oh, hey Deb." Tammy says.

Deb? Monica thinks.

"Tammy, we're all sitting over there." Debra says, pointing to the other side of the cafeteria. "What are you doing over here? Come on so we can catch you up on the *Real World* episode last night."

"Come on Mon." Tammy says, gathering her tray without another thought.

"I think I'll stay here." Monica responds.

"Yeah, that's probably a good idea." Debra replies. "Come on Mon, you don't want to sit by yourself." Tammy says as she holds her tray, ready to move across the room.

Annoyed that Tammy is so eager to leave "their" table in the first place. Monica holds her ground. "No I'm fine. You go ahead."

So she does. Not much of a protest on Tammy's part. It's almost as if she was hoping someone would come rescue her from sitting alone with Monica. Oh well. Popularity does have its price.

MR. B's CLASS – AFTERNOON

The steady hum of the air conditioner lulls half of the class to sleep while the rest of the class follows Mr. B's directions and silently read Chapter 3 of the textbook.

Monica is too preoccupied to fall asleep in Mr. B's class though. Her eyes dart between Johnny and her textbook. He's so cute.

Abruptly jumping up from his seat at the head of the class, Mr. B interrupts the studying and sleeping students. "OK, kids." Mr. B says. "Before you go home today, I've got an announcement."

The students turn their attention to Mr. B, expecting to receive one of his infamous oral exams. Mr. B is becoming known for asking the class to read and then picking random kids to answer questions about the text.

But today, he throws the class a curveball. "Class, I'm going to let you decide what we study." The class responds with thunderous applause. "Not so fast, guys." Mr. B continues. "I'm going to hand you a list of potential topics and I want you and your study partner to pick a topic, research it, and write a short synopsis on why we should add that topic to the final test. Then I will choose the best reasoning and we'll go from there."

Much less intrigued after listening to Mr. B's speech, Monica hardly looks at the list of topics as Mr. B places a copy on her desk. "What about this one?" Johnny says, snatching the paper from Monica's desk. "The link between music and the economy."

"That sounds OK." Monica says. "Why don't we…"

RING! The final bell of the day interrupts Monica's statement.

"Come on, let's get outta here." Johnny says as he snatches his backpack from the floor.

The duo strolls down the hall together and spend the next few minutes talking and laughing. But just as Monica realizes that she's walking down eighth grade hallway with the boy of her dreams, Monica spots The Dolls gabbing near the stairwell.

Jenna fluffs her golden brown hair as she listens to whatever it is that Shannon thinks is so important at the moment. She squints her steel blue eyes and nods her head in approval as Shannon swings her arms around describing some random event.

Shannon is an ultra cute brunette and seems to be the only Doll to have an interest in anything other than fashion. Already geared up for soccer practice, she is sporting a C. Edwards Middle School t-shirt and a pair of boy shorts that she's passing off as gym shorts.

And since she is more toned than she is shapely, Shannon doesn't run the risk of "breaking" the dress code due to over exposure the way some of the more womanly young ladies would.

Erica, whose best attribute is that she isn't quite as mean as the other Dolls, is listening intently to Shannon but she almost swallows her gum when she sees Johnny and Monica walking together. Speechless, her jaw drops and Erica can do little more than point her perfectly manicured finger in Monica's direction.

Lauren locks her sights on Monica and begins to walk over when she's suddenly stopped in her tracks by Jenna's tight grasp. "Johnny Hammond is old news, Lauren. Get it over." Jenna mutters through clinched teeth.

"Get over it?" Lauren says, shocked at Jenna's blunt attitude. "She stole my boyfriend and you want me to just forget about it?"

"You're embarrassing yourself." Jenna says matter-of-factly. "And more importantly, you're embarrassing us. It's bad enough that your little rent-a-man would rather be friends with a has been, than date you. But you make all of us look bad when you shout at him like a lunatic every time you see them together."

Lauren acknowledges Jenna's point and reluctantly turns her back Johnny and Monica. Across the hall, Monica slowly begins to release the tension from her shoulders as she realizes The Dolls aren't going to come over. A few more seconds of peace and she can return her attention her increasingly boring discussion with her beautiful partner.

JACKSON HOME – THAT EVENING

An evening breeze whisks into Monica's bedroom through the window. Monica lies on her bed, staring at the ceiling as the setting sun gradually causes the room to dim. Her mind bounces from topic to topic, never truly settling on one train of thought.

But the one thing that continues to pop in her head is that Johnny Hammond is single. Sure, she feels bad about the nasty break up, but it's not like she did anything wrong. It's not her fault that Lauren jumped to conclusions. After all, Monica and Johnny were just walking together. It's not illegal for class partners to walk with each other.

Of course, most people don't have a crush on their partners. Monica smirks. "Monica Hammond." She sighs. "That sounds so much better than Lauren Hammond."

Monica breathes deeply and turns on her side preparing to catch a quick nap before dinner. Her timing couldn't be worse. "Monica!" Hollers her mother from the stairwell. "Monica, pick up the phone!"

Usually the first person to pick up the phone, Monica didn't even hear it ring. She must have turned off the ringer.

Suddenly her eyes pop wide open and her back stiffens. "What if it's Johnny?" She wonders aloud. Monica hops out of bed and rushes to her full-length mirror. She checks her hair, then her clothes and then her teeth. "OK" she says confidently. Wait a minute. She stops in her tracks. What the heck am I doing? It's a phone call. He can't even see me.

"Monica Jackson!" Her mother yells. "Are you up there?" Monica grabs the phone and puts one hand over the receiver. "I got it!" Monica yells back. She puts the phone to her ear and listens for the 'click' to make certain that her mother hangs up.

Monica closes her eyes and with one last deep breath she says "Hello? This is Monica"

"Hi. Mon, it's me." Says a friendly female voice.

"Oh hey Tam." Monica replies, somewhat disappointed. "What's going on?"

"I've decided that I'm getting rid of my cell phone." Tammy declares.

"At least you have one to get rid off." Monica says. "I think I'm the only girl in school who doesn't have one."

"True, but at least you don't have to worry about Trevor texting you twenty times a day." Tammy grumbles. "It'd be nice if any boy wanted to talk to me that much." Monica says.

"Oh yeah?" Tammy laughs. "Even if it was Chris? He's been waiting at my locker for me before sixth period, everyday for the last two weeks!"

"Wait." Monica pauses. "Skinny Chris or Chris with the bad acne?"

"Number two." Tammy says, holding up two fingers as if Monica can see her through the phone.

"Ah, touché." Monica sighs.

Just then, she hears a light tapping at her door. "Come in." Monica answers. Grandma Jackson pokes her head into the room and pushes the door open. "Hey sweetie." Grandma says. "It's time for supper."

"Hey Tam, I gotta go. I'll talk to you later." Monica clicks the end button.

Monica slouches on her bed for a moment. "On second thought, grandma, I don't know if I'm really hungry." Monica says.

"Uh oh!" Grandma Jackson squeals in her high-pitched voice. "I know what that means. You must be having boy troubles. Am I right?" She says, shuffling toward Monica's bed to take a seat. Grandma Jackson has never had a problem inviting herself into anyone's room.

"More like a lack of boy problems." Monica confesses. "Well tell me all about it." Grandma Jackson coaxes her.

"There's really not much to tell. I like this boy Johnny, but he doesn't even know that I exist."

Grandma Jackson takes a deep breath as she thinks. "Sometimes you have to help a young man to notice you."

"How do I do that?" Monica asks as she props herself up on two fluffy pillows.

"Well I can remember back before your grandfather and I were dating. He was kind of a nerd back then." Grandma Jackson chuckles. "But I thought he was hot to trot!

"So one day I told him that I was starting a study group and that he should join us. Of course, when we met after school, we just happened to be the only two who showed up. And by the end of the afternoon, your grandfather asked if he could walk me home."

"And that's how you ended up getting married?" Monica asks. "There's a bit more to it than that." Grandma Jackson smiles. "But that's how I snagged him."

"Thanks Grandma." Monica says as she leans in to give her grandma a big hug. No matter how grown up Monica tries to be, there's nothing like the love of her granny to make her feel warm and gooey inside.

Monica approaches the next school day as if her life is on the line. Not only does she get up on time for the first time all school year, but she actually asks her mom to drop her off early in front of the school.

Monica practically skips to her locker. After popping the lock she stuffs her homework and notebooks in the locker and grabs her textbook for first period.

Out of nowhere, someone puts his hands over Monica's eyes. "Guess who." Johnny says. But he catches Monica off guard and she reacts by swiftly jabbing him in the ribs with her elbow.

Johnny howls in pain as he falls backwards against a locker. Monica swivels around only to realize that she just injured the hottest guy in school. "Oh my God!" She exclaims. "Johnny, I didn't know it was you. I am so sorry."

I don't think this is what granny meant by snagging a guy. She thinks.

"It's OK." Johnny grimaces. "I'll be fine, eventually." Embarrassed by her actions, Monica instinctively starts to rub Johnny's ribs in an effort to soothe the pain. Thankfully, he smiles at her. "I guess I should sneak up on you more often." He says.

Johnny clears his throat. "Monica, there is something I want to talk to you about."

"Sure. What's up?"

"Well, there are rumors going around that we are dating."

"Really?" Monica says, playing dumb. "I haven't heard anything."

"Yeah. Well there is some truth to the story." He says.

Suddenly Monica's knees get weak. She can't catch her breath and her palms begin to sweat, as thought after thought whizzes through her mind. Is he going to ask me out? Does he like me too? How in the world did I get this lucky? She wonders.

Monica, who always prides herself on playing it cool, contains her excitement. "So which part is true?" She says acting coy. "Well, I..."

"Hey, hey Mr. Lover-man!" Sings Chunk as he crams a few textbooks in his locker.

Charlie "Chunk" Daniels – who is not nearly as fat as his nickname would suggest – is one of those kids who is morphing from the "fat kid" to a mildly handsome and somewhat popular guy. But because he is still a little overweight, he compensates by trying to be too cool all of the time. A feat he just can't pull off.

"Pucker up!" Chunk continues to joke.

Monica ignores his silly taunts. "So you were saying?"

"Oh yeah," Johnny says, obviously flustered. He looks over at Chunk, clearly hoping that he isn't listening. "I um, I..." He stumbles. "I just wanted to say that I do like..."

"I like you too!" Monica interrupts excitedly.

"...Having you as a study partner." Johnny says, completing his thought. "Oh." Mumbles an embarrassed Monica.

"Hey Mon." Tammy's voice breaks through the tension.

"Oh, hey Tammy. Ready for class?" Monica says, giving Johnny a chance to leave. But Johnny doesn't get the hint so Monica forces a fake smile to hide her shame. "Ok, Johnny. You can go now."

"Oh, right." He says, getting the clue. "See ya 'round." Johnny winks oddly at Monica before taking off down the hallway.

"What the heck was that about?" Tammy asks. "I'll tell you later." Monica says.

"Tell her what?" Ebony says, appearing out of thin air. But not only does she not wait for an answer, Ebony ignores the disgusted expression on Monica's face and begins dishing today's dirt.

"Anyways, you guys can tell me what you were talking about later. I've got breaking news!"

Monica and Tammy listen, mildly interested. "It turns out that Johnny doesn't want to date you!" Ebony squeals, pointing at Monica.

Geez, this girl is like Lois Lane. How in the world does she find out all of these things? Monica just found out ten seconds ago!

"My guess is that he's going to go back to Lauren." Ebony rationalizes. "I doubt it." Monica replies. "How would you know?" Ebony snaps.

"I don't know." Monica says. "I just don't think she's his type."

Ebony sucks her teeth. "I'm sorry, Monica. I know you must be bitter because Johnny used you like old toilet tissue, but you shouldn't hate on the next girl."

"Ebony," Tammy interrupts. "Maybe it'd be a good idea for you to let me and Monica be alone for a while."

"Hey, whatev'. Do what you want." Ebony replies. "Don't shoot the messenger."

Monica and Tammy wait patiently as Ebony strolls away looking like a bobble-head doll as she says hello to every single person she passes.

Just then, the first period bell begins to ring, causing a panic of students throughout the hallway. "Crap! We're late." Monica gasps. "No biggie, we'll catch up after school." Replies Tammy. "I've got to go to the library during lunch so I won't see you there."

"OK. Here, take the Boy Book!" Monica says. "I haven't had anything to write in there in like, forever!"

Ah, the Boy Book. Every set of girlfriends used to have one. It's a notebook that girls pass between and during classes that highlights all the latest gossip on the guys in their lives. Sure, most girls tend to just text each other these days, but it's nice to know that these two are still old school.

Monica digs into her backpack and hands Tammy the multi-colored composition book. "Kisses." They laugh in unison, pecking each other on the cheek before they part ways.

Jenna double dips a handful of french fries and washes it down with a low carb vanilla shake. "Whatcha eating?" Lauren asks as she takes a seat at The Dolls' lunch table, joining Jenna, Shannon and Erica. "Oh, the Super Model Special, huh?" She says, answering her own question.

"But of course." Jenna remarks. "It's taco day and I don't eat mystery meat."

"What should I eat today?" Erica asks the crew, tapping her debit card on the lunchroom table. "Just pick your favorite food..." Lauren begins.

"OK."

"...And then put the word 'diet' in front of it and eat that." Lauren laughs.

Erica rolls her eyes. After all, Erica is a very attractive girl and she isn't fat by any means. She just has the misfortune of being a few pounds heavier than the other Dolls.

Jenna can't help but to laugh at Lauren's joke even as she looks jealously at Shannon's full plate of food she brought from the Cheesecake Factory. That girl could eat a cow and still be thin. Jenna thinks.

"Fifth period lunch is so boring!" She complains. "There's nobody even remotely worth talking to in this lunch period."

"I know." Lauren agrees. "You'd think there'd be some cute boys in here or something."

"Johnny has this lunch period." Erica smirks. Lauren takes a sip of her bottled water, ignoring Erica's comment.

"I heard Johnny's dating an actress now." Shannon interjects. "Some girl that acts on Broadway or something."

"Not even! How could he be dating an actress? I just dumped him." Lauren barks.

"He's not dating an actress." Erica says, still tapping her card on the table. "He's dating Monica."

"What?" Lauren screams.

"Lower your voice Lauren. You're going to embarrass us." Jenna scolds. "You've got to get your temper under control. Dolls don't behave like that."

Lauren slumps back into her seat. "Whatever." She sighs. "I just don't get it. What does he see in her?"

"I don't know, but I'm not going to sit around and let Monica steal the spotlight." Jenna says before taking another swig of Atkins. "Do any of you understand how pathetic it looks?"

"Don't get so worked up." Shannon says. "It's not like she's a Doll or anything. And considering what happened last year, I don't think you have anything to worry about."

"I'm not worried about Monica or even Tammy Olsen for that matter." Jenna replies. "They had their chance to become Dolls and they just weren't good enough."

Indeed, Ms. Jenna Arnold turned two life-long friendships into expendable commodities when she backstabbed her way to the top of the school social ladder of C. Edwards Middle School.

Last school year, as spring gave bloom to summer, the buzz over the annual Doll selection began dominating every conversation involving girls ages 11 – 13.

Initially, Mon, Jen and Tam – or the triplets as everyone called them – seemed to be the only girls in the seventh grade that weren't obsessed with becoming a Doll. It's not like the three girls were overly popular, but they were that rare mix of girls who just seemed naturally comfortable in their own skin. Of course it only seemed that way.

Somewhere along the line as girls began to speculate about who would be picked, Jenna's name started floating around as an option. Of course she secretly dreamed of becoming a Doll, but it wasn't until other seventh grade girls started telling her how perfect she'd be, that Jenna actually took the idea seriously.

Why not? Jenna thought to herself. After all, she was cute, slim and she was more fashionable than all of her friends.

Once Jenna's mind was set, it only took a few days of hounding Monica before Jenna convinced her that both of the girls should tryout. Tammy, who was still a flat chest caterpillar, didn't stand a chance of becoming a Doll and she knew it. But with the quite confidence she had back then, she also knew that she was fine with just being Tammy.

That's when it all started. With Tammy tagging along, Monica and Jenna convinced their mothers to take them shopping for a few new outfits. As a gift, Jenna's mother bought the girls' shoes, belts and earrings. They even submitted the standard Doll entry form and 'Who's who' of C. Edwards Middle School quiz.

Yes, there was an entry form and a quiz.

Jenna dragged Monica to all of the little events hosted by The Dolls and the girls sat with a horde of other wannabes and they all listened as Cheyenne – sure to be a future Hawaiian Tropics model, explained, "Only the best will be selected as Dolls."

Then something strange began to happen to Monica. The more she hung out with the cool eighth graders, the closer she got to possibly becoming a Doll, the more she liked it. She enjoyed the 'invitation only' primp parties that were designed to subtly show the girls how The Dolls managed to look so glamorous. She reveled in the chance to sit with the popular girls at lunch. She even enjoyed the dim-witted remarks that the boys passed off as flirting.

The number of contestants continued to dwindle and before they knew it, Monica and Jenna were among only eight other finalists. Word leaked that Monica and Lauren Swarth were front-runners in the competition with Jenna falling in with the mix with the other six girls. This meant that Jenna, who was the one that wanted to be a Doll in the first place, was on the outside looking in.

One afternoon the girls sat around the Spirit Bench as the reigning lead Doll, Constance Bowman explained to her small group of followers, "Dolls can only be friends with Dolls."

Immediately, Monica felt uncomfortable as she thought about Tammy. Why didn't she just tryout? Monica thought. Initially she was upset with Tammy for being such a wimp. She rationalized that it would just be too bad for Tammy if the two could no longer be friends. It wasn't Monica's fault that Tammy didn't want to be a Doll.

That night, Monica and Jenna three-wayed Tammy and tried to feel her out. "Tam, I don't know why you didn't tryout." Jenna barked as if Tammy did something wrong. "Now you're going to be mad at me and MJ when we get a bunch of new friends."

On her end of the phone, Monica waited for a response from Tammy that she could use to blame her as well. But she didn't get one. Tammy simply replied. "Oh, OK." She could see the writing on the wall, but she wasn't going to play Jenna's little game. If her friends wanted to dump her, they'd have to do it on their own. Tammy didn't give an inch.

The next day after school, all of The Doll wannabes sat on the lawn in a semi-circle around the Spirit Bench where The Dolls were seated. When questioned by Constance about whether or not they kicked their "jealous friends" to the curb, the other seven girls proudly began gabbing about how their friends whined and got upset just because they were going to be Dolls. But Monica remained silent.

"What about you?" Asked one of The Dolls who was so naturally beautiful, she looked as if she and her flowing crimson frock stepped right off the cover of a romance novel. "What did you say to that sad little friend that you and Jenna hang out with?"

"I didn't say anything." Monica replied meekly. All eyes were squarely focused on Monica as she did her best to avoid eye contact with any of The Dolls. Monica's face and neck became uncomfortably warm and she tried to calm herself as beads of sweat began to collect on her brow.

"What do you mean you didn't say anything?" Asked another Doll. "I mean that I'm not going to get rid of my best friend just because you say so." Monica said defiantly. Shocked, the other girls gasped and exchanged looks of awe. "Monica!" Jenna yelped. "Are you crazy?"

"No. Apparently I'm the only one here who isn't crazy!" Monica said, rising from her position in the semi-circle. "Only four people here are going to become a Doll." Monica said to her classmates. But all of you just sat around and laughed about how you treated your best friends like dirt! So what do you think is going to happen if you don't become a Doll? Your friends are going to hate you and nobody else will want to be your friend either!"

"Oh shut up!" Constance shouts. "No one wants to hear you cry about some girl who doesn't even matter." She stands tall and hurls her science book into the lap of Shannon Pinefield, who is sitting closest to the Spirit Bench. Stepping over Erica Taylor, Constance comes face to face with Monica.

"Look, Jackson!" She snarls. "The Dolls don't associate with lesbians, losers or lames. And apparently, your little friend is one or all of the above. So get rid of her or you and your out-of-season Old Navy tee will never be one of The Dolls." Constance beamed triumphantly.

Monica's jaw tightened the way it did when the neighborhood bullies picked on G.G. his first day of kindergarten. "I would rather wear last season's Old Navy than look like next season's skank!" She screamed.

The entire audience took one collective gasp! Nobody knew what to say. Even The Dolls were stunned beyond belief.

Jenna watched in horror as Monica snatched her belongings from the ground and dusted off a few blades of grass. "By the way, if you haven't figured it out yet, I don't want to be in your pathetic little group. I'd rather have real friends that like me for who I am." Monica sharply turned her back on The Dolls, whipping her hair in the process.

As she stormed off, Jenna called for her. "MJ!" In her haste, Monica had forgotten that Jenna was even there. So when she heard Jenna call after her, Monica turned to wait for her friend to catch up with her. Jenna jumped to her feet.

"If you go after her," said Constance. "Don't even think about coming back." Jenna stood there as Monica waited for her. Then without another word, Jenna returned to her seat on the school lawn. Monica boldly tipped her nose upward, determined not to let the girls see her cry.

Monica remembers everything about that day. She even remembers holding on to the hope that she and Jenna could still be friends. But that was last year.

"OK class. Time's up." Announces Mr. B. "Put your pencils down and pass your quizzes forward."

Monica looks down at her paper and realizes she daydreamed through an entire pop quiz. Hurriedly, she guesses at as many questions as possible before she collects all of the quizzes passed up from her row. She hands the quizzes to Mr. B when she glances at Johnny and catches him staring at her with the stupidest grin plastered on his face.

"Hey Monica." Johnny says. "Don't you live close to the Farmers Market on Elm?"

"Yeah, kind of." She answers. Actually, she lives a mile away on Peachtree Street.

"Why, what's up?"

"Nothing. I just figured that maybe I could come over and we can get started on our research topic."

The thought of Johnny in her house is nearly enough to make Monica faint. "Um, yeah, we could do that."

"That's the spirit!" Mr. B. says out of the blue. "Hey gang, listen up." He says, waving the quizzes in the air to gain the children's attention. "Monica and Johnny have just set a study date."

Monica's mouth gapes as a chorus of giggles and catcalls rings out from the back of the classroom.

"This is exactly what I want to see out of all of our teams." Mr. B. continues. "You kids need to take advantage of the time you have after school to work together. Be like Monica and Johnny. Set a study date!"

Shut up! Monica screams in her head. Is he deaf? Can't he hear them laughing? Doesn't he know what he's doing?

Mercifully, the bell rings. Johnny hops up and throws his backpack over his shoulder. "So are we cool for Saturday?" He asks. "Yeah." Monica replies. "Just come by around five."

"Sounds good. I'll look up your address in the school directory. Talk to ya later." Johnny rushes out of the classroom leaving Monica absolutely giddy.

After making a pit stop at her locker, Monica heads towards the main lobby when she sees Tammy leaning against the wall of the front office. "Hey Mon!" Tammy shouts. She hugs another friend goodbye and meets up with Monica as they walk out of the school.

"You wanna catch the bus?" Tammy asks.

"Nah. I'd rather walk."

"Sounds good to me. Let's bail." Tammy says.

The girls briskly walk off the school property and up Bleaker Street. As they stroll along, Tammy gabs about changing clothes in gym class and complains about her schoolwork – as if that's important.

Meanwhile, Monica struggles with whether or not she should finally fess up to the lie about her period or whether she should just spend the time bragging about Johnny.

"Hey!" Tammy exclaims, stopping in her tracks. "Let's go to the movies tomorrow night. We can sneak into that new flick about the zombie cheerleaders."

"I don't think I want to see that." Says Monica. "OK, you want to catch the end of Shark Week on the discovery channel?" Speaking in her spookiest voice Tammy says. "Tomorrow night they feature sharks from the deepest regions of the ocean."

Disregarding Tammy's theatrics, Monica begins walking ahead of her as she admits the truth about Johnny. Sort of.

"Tam, I'm going to have Johnny Hammond over at my house tomorrow."

"Get out!" Tammy screams with delight. "That's so cool. Oh my God, you've got to tell me everything that happens." Tammy bear-hugs Monica but notices her friend's limp response.

"What gives?" Tammy asks. "Shouldn't you be about to pee on yourself?"

Monica shrugs and attempts to keep walking when Tammy, who is never the bold one, grabs Monica by the arm. "Hello? I'm talking to you. What's the problem?"

"I don't know. He's coming over to study, but I think I'm a little nervous." Monica confesses. "What's there to be nervous about?" Tammy asks. "If he likes you, that's great. But if he doesn't, that's just fine too."

Monica shakes her head as she in disgust. That is such a pretty girl's response.

Monica studies herself in the mirror. Mac Lip Gloss, check. "Cute butt" jeans. Check. Pink top and matching Pastry sneakers. Check.

Now if there was only something that could be done about her hair. Her dad insists that Monica is too young for many of the hairstyles that she'd like to try; so even when she tags along with her mother to the beauty shop, Monica rarely has anything more than a fresh perm and a few extra curls to show off. Today, Monica's silky black hair is straight and tucked behind her ears, resting just above her shoulders.

She continues to look at herself in the full-length mirror when she picks up a brush and runs it through her hair a few more times. She thinks, not great, but not bad either. Monica checks out her backside. And my butt really does look great in these jeans.

When the doorbell rings, Monica runs to her window overlooking Peachtree Street and crams her neck just enough to see Johnny standing on the front porch. "Ok, here it goes." She says, trying to gain confidence.

Monica flings open her bedroom door and in her sexiest most adult movements, she glides through the hall. But halfway down the flight of steps, Monica's heart skips a beat when she sees her dad opening the front door.

"Can I help you?" Mr. Jackson says, glaring down at Johnny. "Hi sir. I'm here to see Monica."

"Monica who?" Quizzes Mr. Jackson. Thrown off by the question, Johnny looks around for some help. But there is none. "Monica, Monica Jackson." Johnny fumbles. "I'm pretty sure she's your daughter, right?"

"Maybe she is. Maybe she isn't." Mr. Jackson says sternly. "That's not important. Who are you? That's what is important."

Monica stands frozen on the steps, praying that this exchange is over soon. She tries to magically help Johnny outwit her dad. Urging Johnny through her thoughts. Say something smart, you idiot!

"My name is Johnny Hammond, sir." Mr. Jackson eyes the young man with that typical over-protective father expression. "How old are you?" He asks Johnny.

"I'm thirteen. But I'm tall for my age." Johnny assures him.

"Son, you look tall even for my age." Mr. Jackson says, still not impressed. "Now, I could let you in this house, but I still need a DNA sample and a strand of hair."

Monica, about to faint from embarrassment, begins hyperventilating. But just when it seems like her dad is going to ruin her life, Monica's mom comes to the rescue.

"Jerome." Mrs. Jackson hollers. "Leave that boy alone. He just came over here to study with Monica for their social science class." Mrs. Jackson explains, wiping her soapy hands on a dishtowel as she welcomes Johnny inside.

"Well science better be the only thing he's studying." Mr. Jackson says.

"Hi Johnny." Mrs. Jackson shakes his hand and guides him inside, closing the door behind him. "Just ignore my husband. He's been out mowing the lawn today and he got a little too much sun."

Monica resumes normal breathing as her mom directs Johnny to the basement office. Thank goodness for moms. If nothing else, they usually know how to corral a runaway dad.

Fortunately, Monica went unnoticed on the stairs, so she still has a chance to make a great first impression. She checks her reflection in a family photo hanging on the wall as she heads down the stairs to the basement.

Johnny stands in the Jackson family office admiring the computer and the bookcase filled with old thick books. He's very impressed.

He soon takes a seat at the large oak desk and begins playing drums with his fists. He stops short of what would no doubt be a blazing solo performance when Monica appears in the doorway.

His eyes say it all. She looks hot – High school cheerleader hot. "Hi Monica." Johnny says standing up to greet her. "Hey" Monica replies, trying to breath calmly.

"Have a seat." Johnny practically trips over himself as he rushes to pull up a cushy computer chair for Monica. "You have a really nice house."

"Thanks." She says nervously. "I was going to get my own place, but I think I'll stick around here until the interest rates fall a bit more." Monica giggles at her own joke. Johnny giggles too, mostly because he doesn't get the joke.

Changing the subject to a topic he knows at least a little about, Johnny peels open a notebook filled with scribbles that supposedly amount to class notes. "I was reading the textbook the other day and I thought that this might really be a cool angle to present." Johnny says, pointing to a passage in his notebook.

Monica scoots closer to him and acts like she can read his handwriting. It must be the worse scribble scrabble she's ever seen. But this is not the time to point out Johnny's one glaring flaw.

They sit uneasily for a 15 second period that feels like 15 minutes. The room is completely silent. The boy of Monica's dreams is sitting just a foot away from her and there is nothing between them but opportunity.

Suddenly Monica's heart jumps into her throat. Oh my God! She screams inside. He's leaning in to kiss me! Johnny inches ever so close to Monica. Her emotions skip from anxiety to joy as she begins imagining the couple kissing on their wedding day.

Monica snaps back to reality and she can practically feel the heat from Johnny's body. She wants to kiss him now, but she must wait for him to come the whole way. After all, this isn't just any kiss. It's her first kiss. It's going to be amazing. It's going to be beautiful. It's going to be…interrupted.

"Monica!" Mr. Jackson exclaims as his voice cracks. Johnny freezes in his tracks and stares at Mr. Jackson who looks as if he's about to lose his lunch. Wide-eyed and horrified, Monica's father does his best to regain his composure.

"Dad!" Monica yells. "Can't you knock? We're trying to study."

"Study? Is that what you call what was about to happen?" Mr. Jackson marches into the room and grabs a chair from the corner near the bookcase. He positions his chair squarely between Monica and Johnny. Mr. Jackson takes a deep breath as he cracks his knuckles.

"Listen kids, I know what it's like to be your age and to have all sorts of feelings running through your head. I was just like you once." Mr. Jackson explains as he tries his best to relate to the kids.

Not that his words make that much of an impact. Let's face it, grown ups can say that they've been there all they want, but they're so old, there's no way they can understand what kids today are going through. Right?

So Monica and Johnny nod their heads as if they believe everything Mr. Jackson is saying. "You see," continues Monica's father. "You kids are at an age when you're going to have urges...sexual urges. Now that's totally natural." He says turning to Monica to reassure her.

Of course the only thing that could reassure Monica right now would be for her dad to disappear at this exact moment. When she realizes that her dad isn't going to evaporate, Monica does the best thing that a kid in distress can do. "MOM!" She screams frantically, frightening both Johnny and her dad.

"Honey," Mr. Jackson says. "Calm down. It's nothing to be embarrassed about. Sex is a natural thing. But only when it's shared between two consenting adults who happen to be married and can afford to pay for diapers, baby food and daycare.

Just then, a panicked Mrs. Jackson rushes into the room, her hands still soaking wet from washing the dishes. "Monica!" She exclaims. "What's wrong honey?"

Fortunately, Monica doesn't even have to respond. Her mom surveys the situation and immediately deduces that the source of her daughter's angst is sitting right between Monica and this cute young boy. Yes, even Mrs. Jackson thinks Johnny is a cutie.

"Jerome." Mrs. Jackson says in her stern voice. "Leave these children alone." She takes her husband by the arm with one of her soapy hands and guides him out of the office.

"But honey," Mr. Jackson protests "I was just getting to the part about the birds and the bees. I cannot be silence, woman. These kids need to know the truth!"

Monica slinks down in her seat, unable to escape Johnny's shocked glare as her mom escorts her dad to the kitchen. Again, Johnny and Monica sit in silence. Only this time it's much more uncomfortable.

Eventually breaking the ice, Johnny says "Well at least he didn't bring any visual aids with him." Monica herself forces to chuckle. At this point, it's either laugh or cry.

The funny thing is that in ten years Monica may actually be able to look back on all of this and really laugh. OK, maybe not.

"Hey, why don't we get back to our research?" Johnny says, eager to change the subject. "Sounds like a good idea." Monica says. "I'll hit up Google. Can you get the assignment sheet out of my backpack? It's in the corner." Her index finger points Johnny toward her bag.

Just then, Johnny's eyes gloss over, as he reaches into Monica's backpack and pulls out the biggest bra he has ever seen! He marvels to himself. "They don't even have bras this big in the Victoria's Secret catalogue."

He holds his discovery up in the air as he admires its bulk. "What is that?" Monica shrieks in disbelief.

"I think this belongs to you." Johnny displays the bra while grinning from ear to ear. As he holds it tight in his grasp, Monica tilts her head and reads the words "Monica's bra" written on each cup in bright red marker.

"That's my grandma's bra!" Monica gasps. "Gross!" Johnny yells, dropping the bra and wiping the non-existent granny germs on his jeans.

Instead of losing her mind and going on a manhunt for the culprit, who is undoubtedly G.G., Monica calmly says, "I think we've had enough studying for today. It's time for you to leave."

Johnny, sensing Monica's head is about to explode, swallows his giggles and gathers his belongings. He walks towards the office door and smiles at her before leaving. "I'll just let myself out."

"It's all part of my plan!" G.G. exclaims as his mother paces back and forth.

"I can't stand you!" Monica barks from behind her father who is holding her at bay, protecting G.G. from Monica's wrath. "Alright, Monica." Her mother says. "That's enough. Your father and I will take care of G.G."

"That's enough? That little brat ruined my life!" Tears begin to puddle in the corners of Monica's eyes. She can't fight it any longer. Streams of salty tears cover her cheeks. She buries her face in her dad's chest. "When Johnny saw Grandma's bra, he didn't know if he should laugh or be freaked out!" She cries into her dad's tear soaked polo.

"Ha, ha!" Laughs Granny Jackson, who has knack for popping up at the most inopportune times. She slaps her wrinkled hand on her leg and laughs "I'd be freaked out too if I reached in a little girl's bag and saw a bra that size!"

Grandma's joking isn't helping the situation though. Monica is bawling and G.G. is near tears himself.

Without notice, G.G. jumps out of the interrogation seat and sprints out of the kitchen, rushing past Grandma Jackson before she even has a chance to stop him. Monica makes a move to chase after him but Mr. Jackson catches her by the arm just as she reaches the doorway.

"Not so fast, young lady." Uh oh. It's the serious dad voice. Even in her own tornado of tears, Monica wouldn't dare risk throwing a tantrum when her father uses that tone of voice. "Have a seat, honey." Her father says, pulling out a chair from the kitchen table. Monica slumps down in the seat.

"Mother Jackson," Monica's mom says, "would you please excuse us while we talk to Monica in private?"

"Go right ahead." Grandma Jackson huffs. "I didn't want to hear what you had to say to the child anyway. I just came in here to get some prune juice." Grandma Jackson hikes up her old cloth nightgown and shuffles out of the kitchen.

"Monica," her mom says taking a seat next to her. "I know you're embarrassed but I'm sure your brother didn't mean to hurt you. He loves you."

"Well why can't he just leave me alone?" Monica shouts, furiously fighting another storm of tears. She picks up a napkin from the table and dabs her eyes. Sniffle. Sniffle.

"Can I go to my room?" Monica mumbles.

Mrs. Jackson, who has run out of things to say, looks up at her husband. At a loss for words himself; Mr. Jackson nods OK.

Monica takes a deep breath and picks herself up from her seat. "Oh, honey." Mr. Jackson says. "I know I may have overreacted about the whole kissing thing. But you have to understand that I just want you to make good decisions with your life."

"I know, dad." Monica says, still trying to stifle her tears.

"Good." Her dad replies. "And by the way; French kissing is never a good decision. As a matter of fact, just stay away from any kissing that involves more than a cheek." Mr. Jackson says with a smile. Monica rolls her eyes and trots upstairs.

BUS STOP – MONDAY AFTERNOON

The piercing screech of School Bus 13 doesn't even faze the students as it comes to a halt at the bus stop. A group of seventh grade boys fight to get off the bus as Monica and Tammy exit behind them.

This Monday however, Tammy senses that Monica must be in one of her funky moods where she's 'exploring her inner self like one of the college students at the local university. She was tightlipped the entire bus ride and she isn't even paying attention to Tammy's important decision about her toenail polish color.

"What's going on, Mon? Asks Tammy. "I'm fine." Monica begins walking a little quicker down Trinity Street, passing lawn after perfectly kept lawn.

"Well what's with the silent treatment? You've barely said a word all day. What, are you hiding something?" Tammy jokes.

"Wait." Tammy says hoping in front of Monica. "You are hiding something!" She grins. "What is it? Come on. Tell me." Trapped, Monica digs deep into her brain for something to say, anything but the truth about Johnny's attempted kiss and the embarrassment that followed.

"I, I," she stutters. "I haven't gotten my period!" Monica blurts out.

She immediately regrets it. For Monica, the only thing worse than telling Tammy about Johnny's failed kiss, is admitting to Tammy that she hasn't had her period yet.

Stunned, Tammy asks, "You lied?" Monica had completely forgotten that on the first day of school she told Tammy that she had her period. "That's sooo not cool, Mon. We're supposed to be best friends."

"I'm sorry. I know I shouldn't have told you that." Monica says, staring at the top of her white and pink Nikes. "It's just that I'm thirteen years old and I haven't had my period yet. I feel like I'm going to be in college before it happens."

"Relax, Mon." Tammy consoles her. "You're like, the coolest girl in school. You'll get your period. I don't even know why you worry about it." But Tammy's gorgeous smile and can-do attitude only make things worse, reminding Monica of all of her own insecurities.

"I'm not like you, Tam." Monica says walking on. "Boys don't stare at me in the hallway. I don't have huge boobs."

"Are you freaking kidding me?" Tammy laughs. "Do you really think I like being C. Edwards Middle School's own personal Maxim Magazine cover girl? Everywhere I go boys look at me as if they've never seen a girl before. It's creepy. I can't even have a conversation with a guy without wondering if he likes me or them." She points at her chest.

"Tammy, there are tons of women who would love to have a chest like yours!" Monica contends. "Why do you think that so many women get breast implants?"

"I don't know, but I'd rather have someone pay attention to me because they care about me, not my breasts."

Monica turns away, still unconvinced. Tammy's her best friend but since the beginning of the school year, it's been like Tammy represents everything that Monica wants to be. Popular, sexy, and confident. Tammy has it all.

"Tam, you just don't get it."

"No, Monica. You don't get it. You seem to think that I'm some kind of super-woman. But I'm not. I wish I could be half as strong as you." Tammy confesses. "It takes me an hour each day just to figure out what I'm going to wear because I feel so weird in all of my clothes. It doesn't help if everyone tells you that you're pretty if you can't see it when you look in the mirror."

The girls come to a stop at the corner of Trinity and Clermont – Tammy's street. They stand in silence, not knowing what else to say to each other. It's funny how you can know someone for so long and learn so much about her in an instant.

"I'm sorry Tam. I guess I thought that girls like you…"

Monica wraps her arms around Tammy, giving her a spur-of-the-moment hug. "I didn't mean to judge you. I guess we've all got our own issues."

Miraculously, Monica makes it to yet another Friday – everyone's favorite day of the week. After hours of talking on the phone with Tammy about much of the same things that they gabbed about during the school day, Monica hangs up the phone and decides to take in a little television.

But it's not long before she falls asleep while watching videos on 106 and Park. As Monica's breathing gets deeper and her mind wonders further and further into a dream, she doesn't hear her bedroom door creak open.

G.G. tiptoes in unannounced and fumbles through Monica's backpack, which is perched on her white and pink vanity next to her hairbrush. Flipping through a stack of notes and tests, G.G. periodically peers over his shoulder to make sure Monica doesn't wake up.

He rummages though the pockets of Monica's backpack; examining every sheet of paper he can get his fingers on. When G.G. finds what he's looking for, he nearly giggles himself into a silent frenzy. He enjoys his discovery as he gazes at the torn piece of paper with Johnny Hammond's name and number on it.

Not wanting to waste anymore time, G.G. creeps over to Monica's phone, and dials Johnny's number.

"Hello?" Johnny answers.

In a panicked voice, G.G. screams into the phone. "This is Monica Jackson and I have big boobs!"

His shriek startles Monica and she jumps up in bed just as her little brother throws the phone at her.

Confused, Monica says, "What did you just say?"

Knowing full well what he said, G.G. doesn't stick around to answer. He darts out of the room and down the steps to find a safe hiding place.

Monica hears a muffled voice coming from the phone. "Hello? Hello?"

Monica picks up the phone and reads the LCD screen. "Oh no. Please God." She says as she recognizes the number.

"Hello?" The voice says again.

"Johnny?" Monica answers, putting the phone to her ear.

"Yeah it's me. What is going on over there?"

"This is Monica but I don't really know what's going on here." She admits. "All I can say is that it was my little brother that called you. But don't worry. I'm going to hurt him badly."

"Listen, don't get mad at him." Johnny says with a chuckle. "I'm kind of glad that he called. You didn't talk to me all week at school and my guess is that you're still a little bothered by what happened when we studied. You shouldn't be embarrassed. The truth is that I…"

"You what?" Asks Monica.

"It's nothing," says Johnny. "I just want us to be friends."

Here he goes again with that mysterious stuff. At this point, Monica isn't sure if it's cute or just annoying.

"OK. Look, why don't we try this again?" Johnny suggests. "How about I come over tomorrow and we actually do some work? We can compare the notes we've taken so far."

Excited by Johnny's proposal, Monica says, "That sounds great. Come over around six."

Monica begins searching for her meddling little brother the moment she hangs up the phone. G.G.'s hiding place isn't as clever as he thinks. So it doesn't take Monica long to find him wedged between the washing machine and a basket of clothes.

A vigorous assault of Charlie-Horses finally breaks G.G.'s spirit and he confesses that his obsession with boobs is simply part of a plan to help Monica win Johnny's heart. G.G. figures that Monica wants bigger boobs so that Johnny will be her boyfriend. So G.G. has been doing his best to convince Johnny that she is well endowed.

JACKSON HOME – NEXT EVENING

The Johnny Hammond Experiment – as G.G.'s failed attempt to *help* his sister, has come to be known – is put to rest just in time for Monica's next study date with Mr. Wonderful. Like clockwork, Johnny rides up the driveway on his 10-speed bike at 6 PM on the dot. This time though, Monica is standing in the living room peering out through the blinds as Johnny arrives.

Monica is much more casual this time around. Her hair is tied back in a bun. She's sporting a fitted V-neck t-shirt with just a bit of tissue stuffed in her bra to help put the ladies on display. Her worn blue jeans are just tight enough to get someone's attention, but not so tight that her father bursts a vein.

Feeling just as nervous, yet more confident than the last time her would-be boyfriend visited, Monica marches over to the front door and opens it before Johnny's finger can even reach the doorbell.

"Hey Johnny." Monica says with a cool smirk. "Come on in." She takes a step back and gestures inside.

"Is your dad here?" Johnny asks, looking around cautiously.

"Don't worry." She replies. "My mom put a leash on him so he won't bother us. Besides, his bark is worse than his bite."

Wow, that was smooth. Where the heck did that come from? She wonders. Monica is relaxed and cooler than she's ever been around Johnny. It's as if his last visit was just a dress rehearsal. Tonight is the real deal and Monica is ready to take charge and perform.

Although Monica may feel like a Pussycat Doll this evening, she's still just a kitten who lives in her parents' house. And mom and dad say that no boys are allowed upstairs. So again, the cute couple find themselves studying in the basement office.

Monica's boldness carries into their study session. She actually finds herself trying to make eye contact with Johnny. But after an hour of gazing into the hypnotic glare of the Jackson family computer, Monica and Johnny have all but lost the buzz of electricity that sparked between them.

Johnny scrolls through Google as he reads information on the digital music sales over the last decade.

Monica is shocked to see how hard Johnny studies. She never would have guessed that the school jock is also the school geek. She tries her best to conceal a muffled yawn behind the palm of her hand.

"This is pretty boring, huh?" Johnny concedes. "What? Oh, no. I'm having a great time." Monica says in her most annoyingly perky voice before being embarrassed by yet another yawn attack.

"Yeah, you look really thrilled." Johnny jokes. For the first time in over an hour, the two lock gazes. A slight shiver streams through Monica's body as she catches a hint of Johnny's boyish lust peaking from behind his beautiful brown eyes. This could be it. She thinks. He's really going to kiss me!

Johnny begins to lean in towards Monica. Extending his arm towards her, he says, "Monica?"

"Yes?" She whispers, her voice cracking.

"Can you please pass me the blue highlighter?" Johnny asks pointing to the pack of highlighters resting on the desk behind Monica. Unable to look away from Johnny as he leans just inches away from her face, Monica feels around on the desk behind her searching for the highlighters.

Suddenly, like a gust of wind, Monica has a surge of confidence. Her bottom lips quivers as she begins to pucker up. She leans in slightly as Johnny responds by gently dipping his head closer to hers.

Monica can practically feel Johnny's lips on hers when…she begins the longest yawn of her life! Mortified, Monica snaps her head away from Johnny and covers her mouth.

Oh my God! I yawned in his mouth. Monica says to herself. Johnny sits with a blank look on his face, not quite knowing what to do. More embarrassed than ever, Monica jumps to her feet.

"Um, I'm a little tired." She says.

"No kidding." Johnny says jokingly and not helping the situation at all. Monica grits her teeth, suppressing an onslaught of tears.

Johnny gets the clue that this is no laughing matter. "You know, maybe I should let you get some sleep." He says to Monica. "Ok." She says, sensing that the first tear is ready to trickle down her cheek.

Monica spins away from Johnny and rushes out of the basement office. Johnny begins to give chase, but he decides to let her go. This is the second time that Monica's had the school's biggest heartthrob in her house only to be embarrassed.

Dashing up two flights of steps, Monica practically knocks her mother down as she makes her way up stairs. Trailing behind, Johnny marches upstairs from the basement, still stuffing textbooks into his backpack. "Hey Mrs. Jackson." Johnny says with a voice so sweet it can even make a grown woman's knees shake.

"Hi Johnny. Where's Monica heading?"

"She's a little tired." Johnny replies. "I gotta go. Good seeing you Mrs. Jackson." Johnny rushes out the front door, leaving Monica's mom standing in the foyer with a half eaten bowl of butter pecan ice cream and a confused look painted on her face.

Mrs. Jackson locks the front door behind Johnny and heads upstairs to catch a few On Demand episodes of General's Hospital. But thinking back to her daughter's sprint upstairs, she gets that nagging feeling that she's seen that look on Monica's face before. It's the look of a hurt teenage girl. It's the look of a kid who wishes life wasn't so difficult.

So with a mother's love in her heart, Mrs. Jackson takes a right at the top of the steps instead of a left. Pressing her ear against Monica's bedroom door, she can hear the muffled sniffles of her precious little girl.

"Sweetie?" She says in an overly loving tone. "Can I come in?" Mrs. Jackson listens intently for Monica's reply.

The last two years it's felt as if there is always a door between Mrs. Jackson and Monica. A few years ago, Monica was the adoring little princess who wanted nothing more than to be just like her mother, the nurse. But since the middle of Monica's sixth grade year, she's become a recluse and moody young woman that her mom doesn't even recognize half the time.

The two are either arguing or simply not talking. And of course, neither can possibly understand why the other acts the way she does. So Mrs. Jackson has become quite accustom to standing on the "other side of the door" waiting for Monica to let her in, both physically and emotionally.

"I'm busy, mom." Monica replies with just a hint of sorrow lingering in her voice.

"I've got ice cream." Mrs. Jackson says in a singsong voice. Still listening closely, Mrs. Jackson can hear a bit of movement behind the door and after a few seconds, the door handle jiggles and the lock clicks as it's opened. Monica opens the door but retreats to her bed, allowing her mom to let herself in.

Now that she's gained access inside, Mrs. Jackson stands in the middle of the room holding a bowl of melting ice cream. She offers the bowl to Monica. But her daughter doesn't take the bait.

Like most mothers, Mrs. Jackson is clueless about how to talk to her daughter. It's amazing to think that parent's were once kids. There must be some sort of brain zap around age 25 that makes grown-ups forget what it's like to be a teenager.

"Um, so…" Mrs. Jackson mumbles. "That John Hammond sure is a cutie. Do you like him?" Without a word, Monica turns and stares out of the window, secretly hoping that her mom will drop the subject.

Fat chance!

"Dan Wilkes." Monica's mother announces confidently. "What?" Monica asks, finally acknowledging her mom's presence. "Dan Wilkes was the captain of my high school football team." Mrs. Jackson proudly proclaims. Mildly intrigued, Monica shifts around to face her mom. "Was he your boyfriend?" Monica asks, smudging a half dried tear from her cheek. "Yes…and no." Answers Mrs. Jackson. "He was my date for the junior prom. Every girl in school wanted to be his girlfriend."

"And he chose you?"

"Yes." Mrs. Jackson says emphatically. "I may just be a mom, now. But I was really fly back in my day."

"Did you just say 'fly'"? Monica rolls her eyes.

"Anyway, Dan and I went on three dates before the prom." Mrs. Jackson says with stars dancing in her eyes. "So as the prom drew closer, I was really amped."

"Mom." Monica interrupts. "Can you please stop trying to use slang?"

"Like I was saying," Mrs. Jackson continues her story. "When the day of the junior prom came, your aunt Arnetta helped me get ready. It took three hours to perfect my look. But I ended up sitting around and waiting for another three hours." Mrs. Jackson says as the gloom of her memories sets in on her face. "Dan never showed up."

"What?" Monica shouts angrily. "What happened?"

"Well after some encouragement from your aunt, I decided to go to the prom by myself, only to see Dan 'getting down' in the middle of the floor with some other girl. I found out later that the 'other girl' was his ex-girlfriend. They had gotten back together the day before and Dan apparently slipped a note into my locker, announcing that he was taking her instead of me."

"What a loser!" Monica says.

"Trust me. I know." Replies her mom. "But the point is that sometimes things don't always go the way we want them to when dealing with boys. Nobody's perfect. Not me, certainly not Dan and not even you." She explains as she takes a seat next to her daughter. "We all make mistakes and we all get embarrassed at some point. And I'm willing to bet that you are going to be just fine, regardless of what happened between you and Johnny."

Monica's mother embraces her in a way that makes Monica feel like the world is the perfect place it was years ago when she was just an elementary school kid. It's one of those rare moments between mother and daughter that the pair wishes could last a lifetime.

Pulling away from her mom, Monica comes clean. "To be honest, I'm more upset about when could have happened with Johnny than what did happen."

"What are you talking about, honey?" Mrs. Jackson says, intrigued.

"Johnny and I almost kissed." Monica confesses.

"Wow!" Her mom exclaims. "Really? Your first kiss? That's great!" Agitated, Monica says, "Mom cut it out. We didn't kiss. I said we almost kissed. But just listen!"

"Ok, ok. I'm sorry. I'll be quite." Mrs. Jackson says, unable to wipe the smile from her face.

"I wanted to kiss him and I think he wanted to kiss me. But everything just went wrong." Monica explains.

Mrs. Jackson rests her chin in her hand. "Oh I see. You thought it was going to be a storybook moment, huh?"

"Right."

"Well sometimes you have to right your own story and it isn't always perfect. But regardless, just give it some time. If it's meant to happen, it will happen." Monica's mom comforts her.

CAFETERIA – NEXT SCHOOL DAY

Ugh, tuna. Monica inspects the sandwich her mother packed in her lunch. Unable to stomach any more tuna on wheat, Monica listens to the chitter-chatter taking place at her lunch table. But the girls at the table are gabbing about boys and Monica doesn't want to get drawn into a discussion about her and Johnny.

She swivels around in her seat and scans the lunchroom. As usual, everyone is in his or her place. In the world of middle school, very few kids can actually break rank and associate with whom they please. Most people shuffle right over to their snug little group.

A few goths huddle in a far corner of the cafeteria. A group of geeks gather around a chessboard and small group of seventh grade girls who can't put down their compacts for five seconds, primp and pose three tables away. There go next year's dolls. Monica chuckles.

"What up trick?" Chimes a familiar voice. Monica turns around as Tammy takes a seat next to her.

"Hey Tam." Monica says. "Where were you?"

"I had to stay late and clean up the classroom for Mrs. Bellamy. That jerk, Brock Keys kept trying to ask me out during the entire class period." Tammy complains.

Brock is the type of guy that is so slimy that a girl could slide off his face if he tried to kiss her. Every other day he's hitting on a new girl and every other week he has a new girlfriend. He's been chasing Tammy this week but he surprisingly hasn't lost interest yet. It must be the thrill of the chase, because he's getting nowhere fast.

"He keeps bugging me and when I turned around to tell him to shut up, I got busted for talking in class!"

"Sucks to be you!" Monica teases. "Well I'm glad you're here. I…"

"Hey Tammy!" Interrupts a chipper crew of cheerleaders. Ta da! Tammy's newfound popularity strikes again. It's cool though. Monica is trying hard to get used to sharing her best friend. It seems like everybody in school always wants to stop by to say 'hi' to Tammy.

Tammy, however, is still learning how to deal with being eighth grade royalty. Last year she wasn't even the coolest kid in her group of friends. Now she gets invited everywhere by everyone. That's a big jump for a shy sweetheart like Tammy.

Ah, but popularity calls. So Monica plays nice and sits quietly while the group of pom-pom pros gab with Tammy and gush over her vintage jeans and leopard print flats. But Tammy is ready to get back to her friend so she ushers the girls off with a "Ok guys, it was good talking to you. I'll see ya later!"

She takes a swig of her Naked fruit juice before returning her attention to Monica. "Um, Mon, weren't you saying something?"

"Yeah." Monica replies. "It's a little embarrassing, but considering that I haven't been the most honest person this year, I should tell you."

"Tell me what, Mon?" Tammy frowns. "I thought we agreed not to keep anymore secrets?" Monica sighs. "You're right. It's just a little embarrassing. Johnny came over to study again and I think he was about to kiss me, but I yawned in his face!"

"Ha!" Tammy screams, spitting up a bit of her juice. "Girl, I'm sorry. I didn't mean to laugh. But look at it this way; it's not exactly the worse thing to ever happen to you."

Truer words have never been spoken. It was just last school year that Monica suffered through the most embarrassing moment of her young life.

"Everyone sit down and shut up!" Commanded Constance. It was one day after Monica stormed off, leaving behind her chance at becoming a Doll. Emotions were running high as the day for the final cuts arrived. Three random girls who have long since been forgotten were dismissed amongst a whirlwind of tears and red-faced pleas. With Monica out of the picture, the final decisions were pretty easy. Besides, as one of The Dolls would later claim, "those other girls were just here for entertainment."

Jenna, Lauren, Erica and Shannon. The names were announced in that order. Traditionally, the four new girls and the reigning Dolls would all get together at one of the new girl's homes for a sleepover. But with Monica on the mind, there was just one more task to take care of before Jenna and the other girls were announced as the new Dolls.

Constance sauntered over to Jenna and handed her a folded piece of paper. "Here's your assignment. Take care of this and the school is yours."

"Who let you in the house?" Monica asks angrily as she stood in her doorway staring at her ex-best friend.

"Please don't be mad." Jenna begged. "Your mom let me in. I feel bad about what happened yesterday. I don't want to be a Doll if it means I can't be friends with you."

Monica smiled for the first time all day. She invited Jenna in the room and within a few minutes, it was as if there was never a rift between them.

After 30 minutes of talking bad about The Dolls, Jenna came up with an intriguing idea. "Why don't we post a video to YouTube?" As Monica pondered the idea, Jenna whipped out her phone and began recording.

The girls laughed at the expense of The Dolls for a few more minutes, when Jenna said in her best news reporter voice, "Ms. Jackson, tell us who you think is the cutest boy in school."

Giggling, Monica played along. "It would definitely be Mike Tryst. He is so hot, he makes my teeth sweat!" She laughed. Monica threw out a few more random comments and Jenna continued to egg her on until the girls tired of their little game.

The next morning, Monica hopped off the bus thankful that it was the last day of the seventh grade and happy that she and Jenna were still friends.

But as she strolled through the hallways, Monica noticed that a lot of the kids were staring at her. Monica wasn't a wallflower as a seventh grader, but she wasn't a social butterfly either. Something was wrong. What made it even worse is that everyone in the hallway seemed to be in on the joke except for Monica.

The further she walked, the more kids whispered and sneered. Monica neared the school library when a boy's voice from somewhere in the crowed hall yelled the worse thing a girl could ever hear. "Hey slut!"

The mean spirited taunt pierced Monica's ears. The children crammed in the hallway roared with laughter. Monica felt like the whole world was snickering and pointing at her. Confused and visibly upset she began rushing down the hallway towards her locker on the seventh grade corridor.

As she passed the entrance to the eighth grade hallway, Monica noticed Cheyenne and Constance leaning against the wall as Jenna and Lauren laughed uncontrollably.

Monica began to approach the girls but stopped, when someone grabbed her by the arm. "Monica!" Tammy shouted. "Come with me." Tammy dragged her friend into a nearby classroom and away from the taunts.

The girls sat down at a computer and Tammy quickly brought up a YouTube video titled "Monica Jackson the middle school groupie."

Monica watches in horror as the video played back her talking about Mike Tryst and other cute boys she wanted to date. "They sent the link to every email address in school." Tammy said.

Desperate for answers, Monica ran out into the hall to find Jenna. "How could you?" She cried.

"How could I what?" Jenna said. "How could I be friends with a whore? That's a good question."

At a complete loss for words and with her life utterly falling apart in front of her, Monica wanted to disappear. Just then, Mike Tryst walked past her with a few of his buddies.

"You should go ahead and cross my name off the list." Mike said. "Cause it ain't gonna happen!" He laughed.

Monica felt like she was trapped in a bad afterschool special. The entire school was pointing and laughing. She had officially hit rock bottom.

But that was then, and this is now. Then, Monica was a broken little girl who was crushed by her best friend. Now, Monica is a battle-tested young adult who isn't scared of anyone, not even The Dolls.

Well there might be one thing that makes her stomach queasy. That would be a cute guy, especially a guy as cute as Johnny. He can send chills down Monica's spine just by making eye contact.

Of course, the problem with cute guys like Johnny is that not only do they make Monica nervous, but also they are impossible to figure out. At least that's what is running through Monica's head as she sits on the curb munching on a bag of mini Oreo cookies.

She washes it down with a Diet Coke because she's so health conscious.

All the school buses have long since departed from the parking lot, but Monica sits comfortably, waiting for Tammy so they can walk home together. The new and improved Tammy tends to get drowned in a pool of less popular girls who feel the need to verbally vomit all over her with random stories about their own drama.

"Hey Monica!" Johnny yells, sprinting towards Monica and catching her just as she stuffs her face with another handful of bite-size cookies. "Hey" She says, with crumbs falling out of her mouth.

"I know that things have been kind of weird between us, but I need to tell you something." Johnny says. "I wanted to ask you…"

"What?" Monica asks, getting impatient, her soft brown eyes demanding that Johnny finish his sentence. He first noticed Monica's eyes the night that he was studying at her house and they almost kissed, the first time.

"I wanted to ask you if…" He stops again mid sentence. "…if you are going to the Never Land Dance."

The Never Land Dance is the only "social gathering" that is sponsored by the school each year. Everyone's parent's think that it's such a wholesome event, where kids can spend a nice safe evening, while feeling grown-up. And while that's true, it's also jam packed with slow dancing, first kisses and full-blown make out sessions.

The dance owes its silly name to Ms. Drayden the forty something divorcee' Home Economics teacher who oversees the spirit committee. Word on the street – which is just code for Ebony's big mouth – is that five years ago, Ms. Drayden named the dance the Never Land Dance because she wanted to feel young again following her divorce. But despite being named after Peter Pan's hometown, this dance can make or break a girl's image. Showing up to the dance with the right guy can change everything.

"Sure, I'm going to the dance." Monica says, smiling.

"Oh, so do you have a date already?" Johnny says sheepishly.

"Nope. Not yet." She replies. "Oh really?" Johnny's eyes perk up. "Well I was wondering if…"

"Hey guys." Tammy greets the couple. "What's going on?"

"Nothing." Johnny quickly answers. "I was just about to leave." Tammy looks at Johnny with a curious eye. "Ok. I guess we'll see you around."

"OK. I gotta go." He doesn't waste any time jogging away from the girls and towards the outdoor basketball courts.

Boys are strange that way. They barely say anything. And when they do, it's either three words or barely more than a grunt.

But Tammy and Monica don't have time to worry about that. They've got only three weeks before the biggest dance of the school year. Well actually, this is middle school in Brooksville. So this is the only dance of the school year.

CAFETERIA – LATER SAME WEEK

As the days roll by, the school's spirit committee does their best to litter every inch of every wall in the school with green and yellow flyers and posters touting the arrival of the Never Land Dance.

"That new lady in the nail shop completely messed up my toes." Complains Shannon as she stares at the pink and green designs on her feet. "So why don't you do yourself a favor and put your shoes back on?" Jenna scoffs. "Seriously Shannon." Lauren says. "Why would you take your shoes off while were trying to eat?"

Shannon glides her feet into her red flats and begins poking her flounder with her fork. Thursday is fish day in the cafeteria. Lauren gently places her fork to the side after eating exactly half of the food on the tray. She is convinced that the cafeteria staff shovels on much more food than anyone needs. Erica opted for a Butterfinger and a side of hot fries, while Jenna went for the salmon rolls. She's loved sushi ever since the summer when she tried it for the first time.

"Ok, so when are we going shopping for the dance?" Erica asks, wiping the last bit of chocolate from the candy wrapper. "I'm not going." Jenna announces defiantly. "What?" Shannon says, looking up from her shredded filet o' fish. "Well." Jenna says leaning in closer to the other girls.

The Dolls always have to be careful. Everyone in the school wants to know what they're doing and whom they're doing it with. So anytime something important must be said; it must be said cautiously.

"I just don't think I'm going." Jenna whispers with a smirk. "How the heck can you not go to the biggest dance of the year?" Lauren questions her. "Well it's only the biggest dance if we're there, right?" Jenna says. "Well what if we don't go? What if we throw the biggest party that this sorry little school has ever seen?"

"You're gonna throw a party?" Erica squeals. "We are going to throw a party." Jenna corrects her. "I talked to my mom last night and she is totally cool with it. We can have it catered and include invitations and everything!"

Shannon digs into her purse and pulls out a pen and a mini notepad. "Let's make a list of everything we're going to need. This is going to be the best party ever!"

"You got that right." Jenna says. "And more importantly, we will be the best Dolls this school has ever seen.

MALL – LATER SAME DAY

"This is going to be the best dance ever!" Tammy declares as she holds up a black spaghetti strap dress and poses in front of three mirrors in the Macy's fitting room. Monica, draped in a black satin cocktail dress frowns at her reflection in the mirror. It's dress number nine and not one has looked good on her yet.

"Honey, that's a little too old for you." Mrs. Jackson says, approaching the girls with a pile of new gowns in her arms. "I wasn't even going to get it, mom." Monica replies, rolling her eyes. It must be that time of the day when her mom acts as if Monica is still a baby and Monica has to reminder her that she is practically in high school.

"Monica, I just don't want you walking around as if you belong in one of those books, girly girl or something." Says Mrs. Jackson. "It's called Gossip Girl and I was just trying it on." Monica huffs. "I don't even like it!"

Tammy slips back into her dressing room as Monica and her mother exchange glares. Sifting through the stack of clothing she's piled on the pink plastic chair, Tammy comes back to the lavender knee-length skirt that she first fell in love with as soon as she walked in the store. This is still the one and she has the perfect cute black top at home to match.

"Tam!" Monica shouts from her own dressing room. "Can you come here and tell me what you think about this one?"

"I can take a look." Mrs. Jackson volunteers. She jumps up from her seat next to the full-length mirrors in the fitting area. "That's OK." Monica replies.

Tammy pops out of her dressing room and tries to avoid eye contact with Mrs. Jackson while being ushered inside of Monica's dressing room.

It's not that Monica doesn't care what her mom thinks. She just needs a little space. She's becoming a woman and she doesn't want her mom to always make her feel like a little girl.

"That's so cute!" Tammy squeals excitedly, closing the door behind her. Monica turns to gaze at herself in the mirror. She almost feels like a princess. The pink cocktail dress with small ruffles at the shoulder looks as if it was made only for Monica. It's tight, but not too tight. It's grown up, but also playful enough for a young teenager not to look like she's trying too hard. After losing herself in her reflection for a moment, Monica pats herself down until she finds the price tag. Seventy-five dollars. Perfect. She says to herself.

Monica takes a deep breath and steps out to model the dress for her mother. Mrs. Jackson is nearly brought to tears. "You look beautiful, sweetie." Now Monica really does feel like a princess.

"We are so, going to be the cutest girls at the dance." Tammy says laughing.

About a half an hour later, Monica glances to the backseat of her mother's Fusion, just to take another look at her new dress. Fortunately her mom didn't even blink when she saw the price tag. Now if only Monica can be that lucky when her dad sees the receipt. But she can worry about that later. As for now, Monica is just excited to be going to the dance, even if she doesn't have a date.

Monica and Tammy chat about the dance the entire ride. Mrs. Jackson is on her best behavior and doesn't say anything to embarrass Monica. When they finally pull into Tammy's driveway. The slight squeak of the car brakes signals to the girls that they've arrived.

Tammy grabs her bag and hops out of the car. "Kisses!" She says reaching into Monica's open window to give her a hug. "Bye Mrs. Jackson! Thanks again for the ride."

"No problem honey. Tell your mother I said hello!" Mrs. Jackson waits until Tammy is safely inside before backing the car out of the driveway and heading home.

"So is Johnny going to be at the dance?" Asks Monica's mom. Annoyed, Monica stares out of the passenger widow, looking at nothing in particular. Her big bright eyes soak in the scenery of the surrounding neighborhood.

"Honey, I just want to be involved." Mrs. Jackson says as they pull up to their house. "I don't want to talk about it mom." Monica replies. "I'm sure that Johnny is going to go to the dance with some cheerleader or something and I'll be there as the sidekick that no one notices."

"Don't say that honey." Mrs. Jackson says. "I am sure that there will be plenty of boys that are going want to dance with you on Friday. In fact, I'm sure that everyone will notice you."

Monica peers at her digital wall clock from the corner of her eye. "Hold still, baby." Her mother says as she applies the finishing touches to a delicate make-up job. Monica has never worn make-up before. Her dad's rule is that no make-up is allowed until age sixteen, but Mrs. Jackson decided to break that rule today. With a flourishing nursing career and two kids, Mrs. Jackson doesn't wear much more than the occasional lipstick, so she relishes the chance to play dress up with her daughter.

Monica's mom takes a step away from the vanity mirror so that Monica can inspect herself. The soft shimmer of the foundation highlights her cheekbones. The eyeliner gives Monica a sensual look and she immediately feels like...like a Doll.

"You look great honey." Mrs. Jackson beams. "Why don't you go downstairs and model for your father and your grandma?"

"Oh, mom." Groans Monica. She pretends as if she doesn't want to be gushed over. But come on, what girl doesn't? Monica grabs her handbag and glides down the steps to the living room where her father searches CNN.com on his laptop as G.G. and Grandma Jackson watch Wheel of Fortune.

Monica playfully swings her hip and poses in the middle of the room for all to see. "Well look at you!" Whistles Grandma Jackson. "Don't you look cute? I bet all of the young fellas are going to want to make out with you!"

"Mom!" Mr. Jackson shouts, looking up from an article on gas prices. "Monica is not interested in making out with boys."

"Oh, I see." Granny says, chewing on her bottom lip. "I didn't know she liked girls."

"Grandma!" Monica shrieks.

"Mom, that's not what I meant." Says Mr. Jackson. "It doesn't bother me." Grandma Jackson continues. "You ever seen that woman with the real short hair? Ellen DeGeneres? She likes women too. But I still like her show."

Thank goodness G.G. changes the subject. "Are you going to the dance with Johnny?" G.G. asks. "No. We're just friends." Monica says. "But I thought he liked you now. Does he still want a girl with big boobs?"

"Be quiet Gilbert." Mrs. Jackson says as she appears from the hallway. "I told you to stop worrying about your sister's breasts." G.G. puts his chin in his hands as he turns his attention back to the game show.

"Mom, can we please just go." Monica begs. Her mother jingles her keys to she's ready.

"Pumpkin?" Mr. Jackson calls to Monica. "Come give me a kiss before you go." Monica leans into kiss her father on the cheek when he yells "Ah ha! I knew it!" He studies Monica's face. "I knew you had on make-up! You know my rule about make up." He scolds.

"It was my idea, Jerome." Mrs. Jackson said, reaching across Monica to gently push her husband back in his seat on the couch. "She'll wash it off as soon as she gets back, OK?" Mrs. Jackson doesn't even wait for a nod of agreement. She simply smiles in that sly manner that says shut up and please at the same time.

"Come on, honey." Mrs. Jackson continues as she places her arm around Monica and guides her towards the door.

The car ride to the school is like most car rides with Monica and her mom, silent. Mrs. Jackson however, believes in open communication with her children, even if she has to force the communication. "Are you nervous?" She asks Monica, while flicking on the turn signal.

At first Monica pretends as if she didn't hear the question, opting to focus her attention on her chipped fingernail polish. How could she possibly forget to paint her fingernails? "A little bit." She finally answers. "That's natural." Her mother casually replies. "Just try to enjoy yourself."

A line of more than ten cars leads to the front of the school. Car doors open and slam shut as kids hop out and wave to their parents as the parents yell back a bunch of parental clichés about behavior and curfews. The Jackson's Fusion inches closer to the building as parents in the cars ahead drive away, leaving the school administrators at the mercy of their sexually charged, albeit clumsy teens.

As they reach the entrance Mrs. Jackson says "Monica I know that you are nervous about going to your first dance. But I really want you to try to have some fun tonight." Opening the car door, Monica says, "I will, mom."

"Besides!" Her mother calls after her. "What's the worse that could happen?"

Monica follows a bunch of kids into the building and through the main hallway. It's strange being in school at night. The streamers and funky florescent lights that liter the hallways make the school feel like a different place. As Monica heads towards the gym, where the dance is being held, she glances around, hoping to spot Tammy.

"Hey Monica!" Screams Ebony as she rushes out of the girl's room. Ebony isn't exactly what Monica was hoping for, but she'll have to do for now.

"Hi Ebony." Monica says, already feeling like less of a loser now that she's walking with someone else. "Are you here by yourself?" Monica asks. "No. I came with Daniel Gill." Ebony replies.

Daniel must be the shyest guy in school. If it wasn't for the fact that he has to say "here" when the roll is called in class, most people would be convinced that he is a mute. But that is a match made in heaven for someone who talks as much as Ebony.

"I had to pee, but Daniel is still in the dance. Where's your date?" Ebony asks as she checks her face in her compact mirror. It's not like Ebony actually cares about Monica or her date. But Ebony considers it her business to know everyone else's business. So it's practically her duty to ask.

"I decided to go stag." Monica says. "I'd rather dance with whomever I want."

"Ooh, be careful." Ebony says, sidestepping a few seventh grade boys pushing each other around the hall. "You don't want people to start calling you names again." She says matter-of-factly. "I still have a link to that YouTube video. I can't believe Jenna did that to you."

Every word that slips out of Ebony's mouth irritates Monica more and more. She can feel her palms beginning to sweat. "Honestly Monica, if I were you, I think I would have transferred to one of those reform schools for girls with drug problems or something." Ebony clasps her compact shut and pops it in her purse. "But anyway, that is sooo last year."

Monica puts her hands on her hips just to keep from reaching out and strangling Ms. Motor mouth. "How do I look?" Ebony asks, turning to face Monica.

But before Monica can even answer, Ebony is on to another subject. "Oh my God! Did you hear that there is going to be some sort of big announcement during the dance?"

"An announcement for what?" Monica asks as she cracks open the gym doors to take a look at the dance inside. "I don't know," says Ebony while reapplying her lip-gloss. "It's probably a PSA for teenage pregnancy or something like that."

Ebony begins pushing one of the heavy gym doors open. "I'll see ya later Monica. I've got to get back to Daniel. He's always talking my ear off, telling me how cute I look."

Yeah, sure he is.

"See ya." Monica says, hesitating to follow Ebony inside the dance.

Monica scans the crowd from the doorway. The gym has been transformed into a glow-in-the-dark party room. Fake stars, clouds and artificial fog are illuminated by glowing black lights. 80's music blares from the speakers that are propped in each corner of the huge room. This is clearly the work of Ms. Drayden. Monica tries her best to take it all in, however the whole scene is a bit overwhelming.

But Monica takes a deep breath and steps inside the gym. She actually feels a bit more at ease now that she's stepped inside. She gazes upward at the multi-colored banner that reads "Welcome to the Never Land Dance."

Monica glides her hand down the side of her new pink cocktail dress as she searches the sea of faces for Tammy. She smiles and waves at a few friends, but they're already dancing with some boys, so she doesn't bother them.

Standing alone staring at a bunch of dancing couples is awkward at best. So Monica decides to head over to the snack table and nibble on some crackers. While sifting through the crunchy options, she inadvertently grabs for the same spoon as someone else when reaching for the ranch dip. Charlie "Chunk" Daniels smiles at Monica as he hands her the spoon.

"Wow, you look hot!" Chunk says, grinning from ear to ear and thanking God that he had a chance to touch Monica's hand. "Hi Chunk." Monica says, trying her best *not* to start a conversation.

"So, what lucky guy is here with you tonight?" Chunk asks. Monica rolls her eyes. How many times is someone going to ask me that? "I'm not here with any guy. It's just me. I guess I'll see you around." Monica says scooping a pile of snacks into her napkin.

"Wait!" Chunk screeches. "I'm not here with any guy either. I mean; I'm here alone too."

"Oh." Monica replies, working hard to turn him down without actually saying it.

"Do you want some punch?" Chunk asks.

"Well not re…" Smack! Chunk jabs Monica in her left arm.

"Ouch! That really hurt, Chunk!" Monica yells, furiously. "I'm sorry." He says. "I, I was just making a joke." He stutters. "You get it – want some punch?"

Monica gently rubs her arm as Chunk watches helplessly. "Why don't I go get you some real punch?" Chunk asks, sheepishly. "Fine. Whatever." Monica answers, her arm still stinging.

Chunk sprints over to the corner table where the fruit punch is located. For a moment, Monica thinks that she should just dip into the crowd so that he can't find her again. But that would be pretty cruel. All she wants to do is find Tammy and have a little fun.

That's when she hears a friendly voice shout "Mon!" Monica turns to find Tammy navigating the crowd as she approaches. She runs up and gives Monica a big hug as if they haven't seen each other in months.

"Oh my goodness, you look so hot!" Tammy says checking out Monica's outfit. "Me?" Monica acts surprised. "Look at you in that skirt. I bet the guys are all over you!"

Tammy's purple skirt and tight black top made her seem as if she is a senior in high school who decided to slum with the little kids for the night.

"I guess so." She replies. "But I know one guy that would probably like to be all over you." Tammy points at Johnny who happens to be standing nearby.

Johnny's charcoal suit reminded Monica of James Bond. *All he needs is a bad British accent and a chance to save her life.* Monica swoons.

"Go ahead, Mon. Go get you're prince charming." Tammy encourages Monica.

As if waiting for his cue, Chunk appears from nowhere to hand Monica a cup of fruit punch. "Here you go." He says with a smile.

Horrified, Monica doesn't move a muscle. The first thought that crosses her mind is that she doesn't want anyone to think that she came to the dance with Chunk. Her second thought is that she doesn't want anyone to think that she actually knows Chunk in the first place.

Then it suddenly strikes Monica. *Why am I acting like this?* Monica smiles and takes the drink from her suitor.

"Hey! Chunkster!" Johnny says, approaching the threesome. "What up J-Ham?" Chunk replies, trying too hard as usual. The boys fake punch each other repeatedly as Tammy and Monica both take a step to the side to give the guys some space.

"So you and Chunk?" Tammy asks. "I don't know. He just started talking to me." Monica answers, taking a sip of her punch. "Well believe it or not, he's probably one of the cutest guys here." Tammy concludes. "It's like half of the people in the school didn't even show up."

Monica takes a closer look around at the crowd. Tammy is right. Monica can only make out the faces of one or two cheerleaders. There are just a handful of jocks. Absolutely none of the rich kids showed up tonight. And the most glaring absence, The Dolls are nowhere to be found. *What gives?*

"Where is everybody?" Monica asks. "I have no clue." Says Tammy, now picking through the carrot sticks at the snack table.

"This dance is turning out to be pretty weak. But there is supposed to be some big surprise later on." Tammy says stuffing her mouth with carrots and dip. "Yeah, Ebony told me." Monica replies. "So what now?"

"Now we dance!" Declares Chunk. He takes Monica by the hand and drags her out to the dance floor as Tammy and Johnny laugh, following behind.

The entire room is rocking to Beyonce's Dangerously in Love as Monica and Chunk hit the dance floor. Always the class clown, Chunk bumps into three different couples as he makes room to do his impression of Beyonce's booty dance.

Johnny cheers him on, as Tammy and Monica stand by watching. An audience begins to gather to watch Chunk's offbeat booty dance and soon a skinny freckled face boy starts chanting "Go Chunk! Go Chunk!" Within twenty seconds, half of the eighth grade is enjoying themselves as Chunk shakes his groove thang.

Monica joins the crowd cheering on Chunk. All of a sudden the speakers screech and the song comes to an abrupt end as Chunk enters full booty shake. The soft, subtle chords of Christina Aguilera's "Beautiful" begin to pour from the speakers.

Oh my goodness. It's the first slow song of the night! Each boy and girl in the dance clumsily locate his or her dance partners as if they were zapped by magnets.

Monica stands motionless, staring at Chunk and the stupid grin plastered on his face. Chunk takes a deep breath and steps towards Monica to take her by the waist. Monica, trying not to be rude is still not completely enthused with her dance partner and she takes a slight step back, allowing Chunk to hold her hands at arms length as they begin dancing.

"Are you hot?" Monica asks after a few awkward moments. "I guess so." Chunk replies. "My mom thinks I'm hot. Well, I guess she doesn't really say that I'm hot. She usually calls me handsome. But when you think about it, it's really the same thing."

"That's not what I meant." Monica says smirking. "I meant are you hot, you know, like warm? Your hands are sweaty."

"Oh, right." Chunk smiles pulling a ruffled handkerchief from his jacket pocket. "I sweat a little when I get nervous." He says wiping his forehead. Chunk stuffs the damp handkerchief back in his pocket and resumes dancing with Monica, getting noticeably closer than before.

Just then, he leans near Monica's left ear and begins singing off-key. "You are beautiful, no matter what they say." He sings, trying his best to keep up with Christina Aguilera. "You are beautiful in every single way." He continues, growing louder by the moment.

Monica, fearing that someone will notice, pulls her ear away from his mouth. "Chunk! What the heck are you doing?" She says panicked. "Oh, sorry." Chunk apologizes. "I sing when I'm nervous too."

With Chunk's American Idol dreams crashing and burning, the two resume dancing, this time even closer than before. One ballad blends into another and before Monica knows it, she's been dancing with Charlie "Chunk" Daniels for almost three whole songs. Monica is really trying to enjoy herself too; except she suddenly has to pee so badly it feels as if she just downed a gallon of water!

Her mounting bladder issues are distracting Monica more and more as the next song begins. But seconds later, the music is cut short and Ms. Drayden can be heard clearing her voice over the speakers.

The students mumble amongst themselves as Ms. Drayden clears her throat once again. "Attention, attention!" She squeals in her nails-to-the-chalkboard soprano. "We have a brief announcement."

The lights illuminate about halfway, casting a soft yellow glow over the gymnasium. "Where is she?" Tammy whispers to Monica as her eyes scour the room.

"Everyone please direct your attention to the monitor." Ms. Drayden continues. "I'm pleased to inform you that all of the streamers and balloons were donated by one of my favorite students, Jenna Arnold." She says clapping and swooning as if she hopes Jenna will invite her to hang out one day. "Unfortunately, Jenna couldn't be here this evening. But due to her assistance with tonight's festivities, I've decided to play a little commercial that she made just for our Never Land Dance!"

The video begins with Jenna, Lauren, Shannon and Erica sitting side by side on the Spirit Bench.

"Hi, I'm Jenna."

"I'm Lauren."

"I'm Shannon."

"And I'm Erica"

All together now! "And we're The Dolls!"

Sprinkles of cheers and clapping run through the audience. "We're sorry we couldn't be there tonight." Jenna says. "But that's because the Never Land Dance is so lame."

Ms. Drayden nearly falls off her stool. Recovering from her surprise, she frantically fumbles to figure out how to turn off the video.

As bad a Monica has to pee right now, she would love to help Ms. Drayden end this little show. But just like everyone else, Monica is too intrigued by what The Dolls are blabbing about.

The video continues with The Dolls pulling out golden envelopes from their purses. "These are the Golden Tickets." Erica says. "And just like Charlie and the Chocolate Factory, there are not nearly enough to go around." She chuckles.

Jenna smiles wickedly. "Two weeks from today, we will host the biggest event in the history of C. Edwards Middle School. The Dolls' Ball. This exclusive party is by invitation only." Declares Jenna. "That's right." Shannon confirms. "Next week, we will personally hand out the Golden Tickets to the lucky few who we have decided to invite."

The buzz of chatter from the student body grows so loud that it becomes difficult to hear the video. "So get ready for the best party of your life!" Lauren says. "If we invite you, that is." The screen fades to black.

"Ah ha!" Shouts Ms. Drayden as she zaps the video screen off, locating the power button five seconds too late.

"Well that ought to be pretty fun." Johnny says to Monica and Tammy, never giving any thought to the possibility that he wouldn't be invited. Monica sighs to herself. Clearly, she's annoyed with the fact that this was the big announcement that everyone had been talking about the whole night.

"Come on Chunk, let's get something to eat." Monica says, looking to either side for her makeshift date. She looks behind her to find Chunk gaping at her with his mouth wide open.

"What's with you?" She asks. But he's frozen. He can't get one word out. Chunk musters all his strength and simply manages to point at Monica's butt. "What? Is there something on my dress?" She asks, getting a bit nervous. Chunk manages to nod yes. But he still hasn't said a word.

Monica twists around and grabs her dress searching her backside for the source of Chunk's shock. Then to her horror, she sees it. A spot of red. Suddenly freaking out Monica frantically pulls and tugs at her dress, practically tearing the material. No. Please God, no! Monica panics, contorting herself to get a better view.

There it is. Just above the red spot and just below her butt is a dark red streak. "I think I cut you." Chunk blubbers. "You're bleeding."

But she's not just bleeding. She's having her first period – in the middle of her first dance! Now Monica's the one who is frozen with fear. Last year she was the girl on the "YouTube slut" video and now she's going to be the girl who had her period in front of everybody! It's as if the middle school gods hate her.

Monica and Chunk stare at each other. Both of them look as if they're going to be sick. Monica jerks her head back to her blood stained dress, still unsure what to do about it. Should she scream? Should she cry? Who knows? This is her first period! This has never happened before!

"I'm a little scared of blood." Chunk confesses. "Oh, boy. I don't feel so well." Chunk tries to steady himself, but begins to stumble as he shuffles off the dance floor.

Left with no other choice, Monica dashes out of the gym, dodging dancers and wallflowers alike. She can only pray that Chunk doesn't tell the whole world about her accident.

GIRL'S BATHROOM – SAME NIGHT

The cramped quarters of a dank stall in the girl's bathroom is rarely a place of comfort. But at a time when a young girl has ventured into womanhood in front of her entire class, she must find a bit of privacy anywhere she can get it.

Stacie Reddick, a curvy eighth grader with frizzy red hair furiously washes the make-up off of her face as she prepares to be picked up from the dance by her dad. Turning the squeaky faucet off, the rhythmic sound of sniffling catches her ear. Stacie carefully walks to the third stall and listens patiently. Eventually the uneven breathing resumes.

On most days, Stacie can be found gossiping with fellow loud mouth Ebony Ocean. But that doesn't mean that she's a bad person. It just means that she can't be trusted to keep her mouth shut.

"Um, hello? Are you OK?" Stacie questions. Barricaded inside the stall, Monica rips off a few sheets of flimsy toilet paper and dabs her runny nose.

"Go away." She demands.

"Monica? Is that you?" Stacie asks. "I said leave me alone." Monica replies growing more upset.

"OK. I just want make sure that everything is alright." Says Stacie. "Did someone post another video of you?" She asks, part of her hoping it's true. But Monica is determined to ignore Stacie's Q & A session.

All of a sudden the door to the girl's bathroom abruptly opens. Tammy stands in the doorway with a worried look on her face. "Are you looking for Monica?" Stacie asks. "She's in here." Stacie says pointing to the third stall.

Tammy gingerly walks towards the bathroom stall. She's just about to address Monica when she glances out of the corner of her eye at nosy little Stacie. "Can we be alone?" Tammy asks as politely as she can. "Oh, of course." Stacie replies. She walks towards the bathroom door and leans her back against it, holding it open.

Tammy peeks over her shoulder and catches Stacie still lingering around. "I meant, just the two of us." Tammy says pointing at the stall. "OK, Whatev. I was just trying to help." Says Stacie as she lets the door swing shut behind her.

Tammy returns her attention to her sobbing friend inside stall number three. "Mon? It's Tam. Are you OK?" Monica pats her red eyes as she fights to stop crying. "Tam, I just need to be alone for a second." Monica mumbles. "Are you sure?" Tammy asks. "I thought you could use one of these." Tammy slides her hand under the stall door, holding a maxi pad between her French manicured fingers.

But she's shocked when Monica's sniffles burst into sobs. "I can't believe he told you!" She cries. "Who told me, what?" Tammy asks, completely confused. "Chunk! He told you I had my period. Now everyone's going to know that I had my freakin' period in the middle of the dance!"

To Monica's surprise, her best friend starts laughing. "Chunk didn't say anything! He's sitting in the corner sipping cold water. Mon, I knew what happened as soon as you ran out of the dance. Remember, I'm the girl who had her first period while waiting in line to ride the Batman rollercoaster at Six Flags."

"So nobody knows?" Monica asks, her crying tapering off into a whimper. "I don't think so." Tammy says. "Now take this stupid pad." She dangles the maxi pad under the stall door again and Monica grabs hold of it. "You know how to use it, right?" Asks Tammy.

"Yeah, my mom showed me a while ago. But what about my panties and my dress?"

"Here." Tammy flings a sweater over the top of the stall. "I stopped by my locker and picked it up. Tie it around your waist and no one will even notice. I'm not sure what you can do about your underwear. I guess you can put it in your purse and wash 'em when you get home."

That sounds good enough to Monica. She stuffs her soiled panties in her purse, takes a deep breath and opens the stall door.

"Thanks Tam." Monica says softly. Monica washes her hands with soap and cold water. She splashes her face three times still hoping that this is a dream and not another embarrassing chapter in her life at C. Edwards Middle School. "I'll call my mom." She mutters. "Already done." Tammy smiles, waving her cell phone. "I thought you'd want to get out of here, so I specifically asked for your mom to pick us up."

Monica begins to breakdown again. She hugs her best friend tightly, and cries in her arms. We should all be so lucky to have a friend like that.

Monica meets the following Monday morning with fear. Despite spending the weekend listening to her mother's soothing words, Monica is convinced that both the eighth and seventh grade classes will be waiting in the parking lot to ridicule her. The period princess: that's what they'll call her. Or maybe it will be something clever like Monica "Maxi Pad" Jackson. Monica is sure that the nickname Maxi will be hers for the rest of her life.

When she arrives at school Monica quickly realizes that she was right about one thing. The school is buzzing. But her name cannot be found anywhere on the lips of the adolescent chatter boxes roaming the hallways. Everyone's conversations are consumed with talk of The Dolls' Ball.

From cheerleaders to the debate team, no one seems immune to the intoxicating idea of being one of the chosen few to receive a Golden Ticket. It's clear that an invite to this party can change your social standing in a heartbeat. Outcasts can become the in-crowd and queens can become commoners all at the whim of Jenna and her devoted sidekicks.

"I think I'll get an invite. Jenna always laughs at my jokes in gym class." Remarks a frumpy looking girl.

"I hope Lauren isn't still mad about me wearing the same outfit as her last week." Frets another girl.

Even the teachers can be overheard speculating about the grand scale of the event. "I heard that they've hired a rock band." Gabs Ms. Drayden to another teacher.

Monica strolls the halls clutching her textbooks and cringing at the oversaturated rumor mills of C. Edwards Middle School. But on second thought, maybe this isn't so bad. Monica smiles. If everyone is caught in Jenna's web, no one can possibly be concerned with Monica's little accident.

As she fiddles with her locker combination, Monica can't help but to smile even more. She's been so distracted by the possible embarrassment of her first period that she forgot that this should be something to be happy about. She's been waiting for her period since she was eleven years old for goodness sake.

"Hey trick. What are you so happy about?" Tammy says slumping against the neighboring locker, her bouncing midnight mane, draped over her shoulders. "Oh nothing." Monica replies. "Just the fact that I am a woman, now." She says beaming.

"Here hold these." Monica piles her textbooks into Tammy's arms. "I always have the worst time with this stupid combination." Monica says, popping open her locker. She swings her backpack off her shoulder, glances to either side, and pulls out a mega pack of pads and jams it into her locker.

"A 64 pack!" Tammy exclaims. "I didn't even know they made 'em that big!"

"Shut up, Tam. I don't want the whole school to know!" Monica says, slamming her locker.

"Well why the heck did you buy every pad in town?"

"It's my mom. She buys them from the hospital when ever they have extras." Monica holds her backpack open as Tammy dumps Monica's books inside.

"Well unless you plan on having your period everyday for the rest of the year to make up for lost time, I don't think you'll need that many." Tammy jokes. "Funny." Monica smirks as the girls begin to stroll the halls.

"I just hope that Chunk doesn't say anything."

"Yeah, right!" Tammy laughs. "He's probably still sitting in the gym wondering what happened!"

The girls continue gabbing as they stand outside of Tammy's first period class until the first bell rings. "Don't forget to write to me in the Boy Book." Monica says.

Tammy whips out the pink and green notebook. "I took care of that last night." She smiles. "So what did you write about?" Monica asks impatiently. "Read the book, genius." Tammy says, backing into her classroom. "I'll see yeah later." Monica stuffs the notebook into her backpack. "See ya!"

"Of course the dance was lame." Monica overhears Shannon Pinefield chatting with a mildly cute brunette. Shannon is the only Doll in Monica's Spanish class. By default, that makes her the most popular girl in class. All of the girls who would pay to carry Jenna and Lauren's dirty gym clothes get a glimpse into the glam world of The Dolls just by listening to Shannon's rants.

"Let's be real. Our party is going to be way better than any silly little dance anyway." Shannon brags. The brunette asks "Is it true that there's going to be a big time rapper?" Shannon flashes a trademark smirk. "You'll find out for yourself. If you get invited." She says ending the conversation probably because she has no clue what's going to happen, herself.

"But like I was saying. I'm not surprised that the dance sucked." She says again.

After listening to Shannon's self-indulged babbling, Monica actually considers paying attention to Senora Cardoza's lesson today. But the feeling doesn't last long and Monica flips open the Boy Book instead of following along in Chapter Four - *Conjugating Spanish Verbs*.

Mon,

So sorry 'bout the ur bloody booty. LOL! Had 2 joke u. Don't feel bad. Ur all grown now. Anywho, U won't believe the crap at the Dance. First of all, every guy I danced with smelled like he took a bath in Old Spice. And nun of em were cute. Who cares about being popular if u can't find a friggin' date!

Monica plops her chin in her palm and stares at her textbook as if she's following along closely. She doesn't give much thought to Tammy's pretty girl problems. Instead, she tries to figure out what her next move should be with Johnny. But the shrill clanging of the first period bell jars Monica from her thoughts. The period is over already? Yikes, time really flies when you're plotting on boys!

Monica safely tucks her belongings into her backpack and files out of the classroom with the rest of the students. Nearly everyone continues to gab endlessly about The Dolls' Ball.

Ebony was overheard telling some kids that MTV was going to film the party. There was another rumor floating around that The Dolls were only inviting high school kids so that they could be the most popular girls in high school before they even get to ninth grade.

The library is practically the only place in the school that isn't overrun with talk about The Dolls. So Monica decides to skip lunch for the safe haven of the computers that line the wall of the school library. She should be able to find something worth reading about on Yahoo!

The rest of the school week has no shortage of party talk. And it seems that no one is safe from the spell casts by The Dolls and their blow out: No one except Monica. She's convinced that The Dolls have no plans to include her in the biggest bash of the year.

As Friday rolls around the rest of the students at C. Edwards can exhale at last. Today The Dolls will pass out the coveted Golden Tickets.

"Each ticket has a name printed on it." Jenna explains as she fans herself with a handful of the slick shimmering envelopes containing the tickets. "They only admit one person, no guests."

Shannon, Erica and Lauren primp and pose on either side of Jenna on the Spirit Bench, which is currently plastered with the blue and gold logo of the C. Edwards Hawks. A crowd of almost seventy students gathers during fifth period lunch.

Sporting a pair of suede Jimmy Choos, a plaid mini-skirt, a white tee and vintage denim jacket; Jenna stands to address her audience further. "Most people are not going to be invited to this party. That's why it's called 'invite only.' She says using finger quotes. "So don't beg us for an invitation if we don't give you one. If we left you out it's because we meant to. We didn't forget. We didn't make a mistake. We just didn't invite you."

Lauren snickers to herself while admiring her fresh manicure. "And the tickets are non-transferable." Lauren adds, brushing a piece of lint from her flower print skirt.

Jenna takes her seat next to Lauren and holds out the envelope containing the tickets. Erica and Shannon jump to their feet and Erica takes the tickets. "Quiet please." Says Shannon. "We're going to begin calling names. If your name is called, please come get your tickets and step to the side."

The horde of students waits anxiously for Erica to call the first name. A group of seventh grade girls jockey for position – as if they actually have a chance of being invited. A few husky football players mull around the back of the group, trying to act nonchalant while listening for their names to be announced.

Erica clears her throat and glances at the first envelope. "Deana Jones?" She says, surveying the crowd for the first recipient. Deana, a chubby fashionista known as much for her sharp tongue as her stylish couture, waltzes to the front of the crowd and hugs Jenna and Erica before accepting the invitation. She smirks at the jealous onlookers as she saunters off to brag to anyone who will listen.

One by one, Erica rattles through 19 other names before she runs out of tickets. Many of the kids have slipped into the background, disappearing before it becomes all too obvious that their names will not be called. Some students however, stick around, praying that by some act of God, their name will be among the last ones.

Better luck next time!

"That's all of the ticket's we have for now." Erica announces with a plastic smile. "Everyone else that we picked is not in this lunch period and we'll hand those tickets to them personally."

As if the kids at school weren't obsessed before, the entire student body is frenzied for the remainder of the day. Each time The Dolls honor another one of the chosen few with a Golden Ticket it sends ripples throughout the social hierarchy of the school.

Monica stares blankly into her locker as she tries to ignore Ebony and Stacie's ecstatic squeals of joy as they bounce around in a circle, holding each others hands and waving their Golden Tickets.

Monica rolls her eyes and tucks her hair behind her ear as she closes her locker. That's so immature. She thinks to herself as she sidesteps the giddy duo.

Clutching her textbook, she heads towards Mr. B's class. As she's walking upstairs to the second floor, she catches a glimpse of a group of boys surrounding a girl. It must be Tammy.

Monica pokes her nose into the small cluster. "Hey Tam!" Monica says. "Hey Mon! You headed upstairs? Wait up!" Tammy says excusing herself from her admirers with a seductive wink.

"Thanks for the search and rescue." Tammy says to Monica as they skip up the steps. "What do guys expect you to do when they just huddle in a circle like little puppies?"

Monica smirks. "If it ever happens to me, I'll let you know what I figure out."

"Well at least that Golden Ticket nightmare is over with." Tammy says, changing the subject. "I swear I'm going to vomit if another girl acts as if she just won the lottery just because she got invited."

Monica chuckles to herself. "I know. I think I'm going to choke the next girl who screams 'Oh my God, I was invited!'"

"Tammy Olsen!" A booming voice fills the air. The startled girls turn around to see Gravy Train Gary standing across the hall.

Gravy Train Gary or G-train as he is called by his co-hosts, is a morning talk show host on hot 91 FM. He's known for his crazy on-air antics and his thunderous voice. Yeah, he's just a local guy, but he's still a mini celeb in Brooksville.

Tammy and Monica stop in their tracks just as Gary approach with The Dolls just a few steps behind. "T-t-t-Tammy!" Gary yells excitedly. "Congratulations! You have been hand selected by Jenna, Lauren, Shannon and Erica to attend the biggest party in the history of this school!"

Shocked, both Tammy and Monica stand dumfounded staring at Gary. Jenna takes the Golden Ticket from the radio host and offers it to Tammy. "Tam, this is the last Golden Ticket and it has your name on it."

Tammy gently takes the invitation from Jenna. She grips it tightly, staring at her name printed in bold letters. She wants it. But it's not just the ticket she wants; it's the validation. It's the proof that she matters to everyone in the school. It's the symbol that she's not the wallflower who was always the third wheel even in her own group of friends.

Monica watches Tammy's eyes, fully expecting her to breakdown in gratitude at any moment. Tammy slides the Golden Ticket between her fingers, her eyes affixed on her name printed on the front.

"Am I really invited?" Tammy asks, looking up from the ticket. "Of course, Tam." Jenna answers. "Let's face it. You're one of the most popular girls in school. Everyone loves you! And besides, we used to be like best friends. I don't see why we can't hang out anymore."

Monica is burning up inside. She can't believe the nerve of Jenna. But what's even worse? Tammy is actually considering this! Monica wants to smack them both.

"I can't believe you really want me to come to the party." Tammy says still shocked. "What can we say?" Lauren interjects. "It's your lucky day!"

Jenna smiles and gives Tammy a hug, still completely ignoring Monica. "She's right Tam." Jenna says. "Just say thank you and call me this weekend to talk about what to wear."

"Thank you?" Tammy questions meekly.

"Should I say thank you for the way you turned your back on me last year?" Should I say thank you for the way you ditched me and Monica just so you could join this pathetic group of wannabes?" Tammy asks getting angrier with each syllable. "Or maybe I should say thank you for helping me to realize what a selfish, evil, attention whore you really are!" Tammy yells, seething with anger.

"Excuse me." Gary interrupts. "I don't really do girl fights, so if I'm going to be asked to referee, I'll have to charge you extra." He says, turning to any one of The Dolls for some sort of clue.

Jenna ignores Gary, "I'm the one who wants all the attention? You and your sad little friend are both the same!" She says, pointing at Monica. "Neither of you can stand the fact that everyone in the school wants to be like me. You're both jealous because I'm a Doll and you're not!" Jenna screams.

"You know, you're right about one thing." Monica says, diverting Jenna's anger towards her. "I wanted to be a Doll. But as much as I wanted to be one of the most popular girls in school, I realized that it wasn't worth hurting my friends. Because at the end of the day, friends are not just people that dress alike and talk alike. Friends are people that really care about you and want you to be happy."

Monica takes Tammy by the hand. "Come on Tam. Let's go." But Tammy pulls away briefly. "One more thing, Mon." Tammy rips the Golden Ticket into fours and let's the pieces gently fall to Jenna's feet. An irate Jenna fights back tears as Monica and Tammy turn their backs and leave.

Monica pulls her pink and green sheets above her head as if it will drown out the sound of knocking on her bedroom door. "Who is it?" She mumbles, unable to ignore the annoyance any longer. "It's me!" Her little brother announces. "Mommy says that someone is on the phone and wants to talk to you!" He continues.

Squinting under the glare of the sun's rays, Monica grabs her clock and pulls it within inches of her face as she tries to see the time. Eight thirty? She says to herself. Who in the world is calling this early on a Saturday morning?

Monica tosses her clock back onto her nightstand and fumbles with her phone. "I got it!" She yells. As usual, she waits to hear her mom hang up the other phone before speaking. Click.

"Hello?" Monica says. "Hey Monica! I hope I didn't wake you." Johnny says. "No, not at all." She lies as she heaves her sheets to the side and clears her throat. It's very hard to sound cute when you're half asleep.

"What's up?" She asks.

"Nothing, really. I just called to see how my study partner is doing."

"Oh, I'm fine…I guess." Monica says.

Unsure of what to say next, the two of them sit for a few long seconds listening to each other breathe. "So…was that it?" Monica asks, breaking the silence.

"Um, well, not really." Johnny mumbles. "I was wondering if you're going to The Dolls' party. I heard it's going to be crazy! "

"I wasn't exactly invited." Answers Monica. "What?" Johnny says surprised. "Oh, right." It finally dawns on him. "I guess I forgot about Jenna and that whole YouTube thing."

"And I'm not particularly good friends with Lauren, Shannon and Erica either." Monica replies. "You know, I don't get it." Johnny says frustrated. "From what I hear, you and Jenna used to be best friends. Why can't you two just make up?"

Monica wonders the same thing every time she flips through an old photo album stuffed with pictures of her, Tammy and Jenna at the mall, at Disney World, at the hair salon and any other place a bunch of girls would find themselves.

"It doesn't matter." Monica laments. "Even if Jenna and I were friends again, it wouldn't be the same. She's so different now. She's just so...so..."

"Evil." Johnny interrupts. "Cruel. Rude. Wicked. Stop me if I'm getting warm." Monica can't help but chuckle at Johnny. Anyone of those words would perfectly describe Jenna, the queen of mean.

"If you think she's so bad," Monica says. "Why are you going to her party?"

Johnny let's a deep sigh as if he's mulling over a math equation. "I don't know." He says. "I guess I'm going because all of my friends are going. It's the biggest party of the year. Everyone is going to be there. Well, almost everyone."

Monica lays her head back down onto her overstuffed pillow and clutches the phone tight against her head. "It's just not fair." She complains as if she's talking to one of her friends and not the hottest boy on the planet. "Why does Jenna get to decide who is popular and who isn't?"

"I don't think it's that simple." Johnny says. "I mean, some people that were nerds last year are really popular this year. And some people that were popular are kind of like the school outcasts, now. It happens all the time." Johnny begins to laugh aloud. "It could even happen to The Dolls."

Her eyes widen and Monica starts grinning uncontrollably. "You know what? You're right!" She says to Johnny. "I've gotta go."

"But we're still talking." He protests. "We'll talk on Monday!" Monica says hanging up on him.

"It could even happen to The Dolls." Monica smirks.

Staring through her reflection in the Plexiglas frame of the vending machine, Jenna debates the nutritional value of Hot Fries versus M&Ms. Hmm, decisions, decisions. She presses D7 and watches as the milk chocolate candies fall to the bottom of the machine where she snatches them up. She looks over her shoulders to see if anyone is keeping tabs on her.

"Oh my God!" Exclaims Erica as Jenna takes a seat across from her with the M&Ms in one hand and a diet coke in the other. "What's with the meal? You only drink diet coke with M&Ms if you're stressed out."

Biting the corner of the package of candy Jenna rolls her eyes. "I'm fine." She says as she spits out the bit of torn wrapper.

"Yeah, likely story." Lauren chimes in. "Pop a few more bags and you'll start looking like Ugly Betty." Shannon and Erica laugh briefly before Jenna's piercing glare sets them straight. "Maybe you should stop worrying about me, and concentrate more on your dry skin." Jenna remarks to Lauren while popping another candy into her mouth. "I hear Proactive is having a sale."

Ouch! Shannon and Erica don't know whether to laugh or duck for cover. Defeated, Lauren breaks her gaze with Jenna.

"This party has to be perfect." Jenna declares to no one in particular. "Don't worry." Shannon says. "My parents paid for the sushi chef on Friday. He'll be mixing up all sorts of rolls and such all night!"

"Good. My parents have already ordered all of the gift bags and party planner has all of the decorations." Says Jenna before taking a swig of diet coke. "Too bad someone didn't get The Tough Luck Band like she promised."

"My dad said they cost like a hundred thousand dollars!" Lauren explodes, trying to defend herself.

"I'm so sick of your excuses!" Jenna snaps back. "You shouldn't have promised something if you couldn't deliver. This is going to be the biggest day of our lives and everyone else at this table did her job. The least you could do was get one stupid band!" Jenna tosses her half-eaten bag of candy to the side in disgust.

"Did you get anyone to perform?" Erica asks, trying not to cause too much of a stir. "Not yet." Lauren answers, suddenly to afraid to make eye contact with any of the girls.

"Not yet?" Jenna repeats. "I'll tell you what." She says, grabbing Lauren's milk, chips and apple from the table and slamming them back onto tray. "Until you find someone to perform, Ms. 'we should get The Tough Luck Band,' go sit somewhere else!" Jenna screams.

"But you can't do that!" Lauren cries. "I'm a Doll. I can't sit with anyone else!"

"Then go sit by yourself!" Jenna snarls.

"Jenna, please, you can't do this to me." Lauren whispers. But Jenna turns her head, refusing to further acknowledge her so-called friend.

"Guys, come on." Lauren pleads, turning her attention to Shannon and Erica. "We're The Dolls. Don't act like I'm some loser! What are people going to say if we don't sit together?"

Erica begins fiddling with her food, trying to ignore Lauren. Shannon, however, doesn't feel quite as bad. "You should go." She says in her most deadpan voice.

Still in denial, Lauren just keeps looking to each of the girls for some sort of sign that this is just a cruel joke. But their faces say otherwise. Fighting back a storm of anger and tears, Lauren slings her Louis Vuitton bag over her shoulder, picks up her lunch tray and marches off to find another place to finish her lunch.

The Dolls watch Lauren slink away. "Did we have to make her leave?" Erica asks. "Yes." Jenna replies firmly. "I'm not going to look stupid because she couldn't take care of her part of the bargain."

"But Jen," Erica says, "Everybody loves you."

"Don't call me 'Jen,' OK?" Jenna says. "That's the type of nickname a Sevie would have." She reasons.

"Sevies," for those that don't know, are what eighth graders at C. Edwards call seventh graders.

"We are the sisters of Delta Omega Lambda." Jenna continues. "But if we don't start acting like it, someone like Tammy Olsen is going to run this school. And I'm not about to let that happen."

Sunlight beams down on Lauren through the library's large bay windows as she bides her time, trying to go unnoticed. Terrified that rumors will begin to swirl if she eats her lunch by herself or with another group of girls, Lauren dumps her lunch and is spending the remainder of the period in the school library acting as if she's studying.

But pretending to drown in a sea of prose by Richard Wright and James Baldwin is no easy task for a debutant who spends about as much time reading books as Lindsay Lohan spends in a soup kitchen. So not long after Lauren takes her seat in the library, her eyes begin glaze over.

"OMG!" Ebony shrieks, stopping abruptly in front of the double doors leading into the library. "Is that Lauren Swarth?" She gasps. "I think you're right!" Says Stacie, who practically trips over her loudmouthed buddy. "What is she doing?" Ebony wonders aloud as the girls gawk from the doorway as if they're watching an endangered species. "It looks like she's reading." Stacie says, confused. "Maybe she's taking a mini Dolls vay-k."

The two girls bounce theories back and forth for a few seconds. Eventually, they change the subject and agree to ditch the rest of fifth period in favor of a Taco Bell run. However, the rumor mills don't stop for lunch breaks. So the duo skips school and still finds time to whip out their iPhones to text anyone in school with a pulse. In fact, by the time Ebony scarfs down her greasy-good Nachos Bel Grande 20 minutes later, Lauren herself gets a text on her Blackberry from Reese Trenton, a seventh grade opportunist who will do anything to be one of next year's Dolls.

R U OK? I heard u were in the bathroom crying b/c Johnny is n luv with Monica! Did Jenna really say that u deserved what u got? Don't feel bad. Gurlz can be so mean. I think ur the best! CUL8R!

"What?" Lauren screams, alarming the students studying at the table next to her in the process. The frumpy librarian glances over the top rim of her bifocals and motions for Lauren to hush up.

Lauren snaps her compacts close and stuffs her fashion magazines in her bag as she fumbles around trying to pack her belongings. Flustered, she doesn't even notice when her phone tumbles to the floor while she is in the midst of cramming everything in her bag.

"Got what I deserve?" She mutters. "I can't believe her!" Lauren storms out of the Library. "Outta my way!" She yells as she brushes past Monica who has the misfortune of walking into the library as Lauren makes her fierce exit.

Monica's first inclination is to turn around and grab Lauren by her hair and drag her around the library kicking and screaming. And although that would definitely be fun, Monica has a reason for coming to the library today and she won't be distracted by a Taylor Swift wannabe.

But she can be distracted by something else! What's that? Monica thinks as she comes to an immediate halt. Lauren's jewel encrusted Blackberry lies helpless on the floor beneath a table.

As nonchalantly as she possibly can, Monica strolls over to the table and places her backpack on a chair. She scans the room to make sure no one notices as she bends down and scoops up the phone, slyly dropping it in her backpack. Oops!

Does Monica know what she did is wrong? Yes. Does she realize that she should track down Lauren and give her the phone? Yes. Does she care? No.

Instead of debating the moral dilemma of 'borrowing' Lauren's cell phone, Monica marches towards an empty computer – which was her original destination in the first place.

But just as Monica sits down at a computer to Google "best ways to get revenge," she peers into her backpack at Lauren's phone. She discretely slips the phone out of her bag and begins scrolling through Lauren's private information. Phone numbers, text messages, and emails: it's all here.

"I don't get it." Tammy sighs as she brushes her hair, focusing on her reflection in the bathroom mirror. Monica chucks her backpack to the floor in front of an empty stall when she remembers how gross the bathroom floor is and quickly picks up the bag and places it on the sink in front of the mirror. "What do you mean you don't get it?" Monica says, pausing to check her own hair.

"I mean; I don't even want to throw a party. So why would I have one on the same night as the biggest party of the year?" She asks, shoving her brush into her purse.

"Jenna's party isn't going to be so great after all." Monica replies. "How do you know?" Tammy asks.

"Let's just say that I've got some inside information." Monica smiles. "And besides, when The Dolls party goes south, where are all of the kids going to go?"

"I don't know, home, I guess." Tammy sighs.

"No! They're going to go to your party!" Monica squeals. "Why would anyone want to come to my party?" Tammy asks.

"Tam, everybody loves you." Monica says convincingly. "I wouldn't be surprised if your party is bigger than The Doll's Ball anyway." She continues now unconvincingly.

"Fine." Tammy gives in. "We can do it Friday. But you'd better help me host it. That way, if it's lame, we both take the blame."

Just then, the bathroom door squeaks close and a chill runs down Tammy's spine as she realizes that someone just overheard the girls talking. That someone? It's none other than the unmatched middle school mouth, Ebony.

"You're going to throw a party on the same night as The Dolls?" Ebony asks gleefully, pulling two cell phones out her handbag. "It's just a little get-together." Tammy says, trying to cover her tracks. "No it's not." Monica interrupts.

"Tammy's party is going to be the best party that this school has ever seen! Even The Dolls will want to come to her party." Monica folds her arms across her chest, smirking with pride.

Ebony gasps at Monica. Smirking with glee, Monica snatches her bag from the sink and heads towards the door. "You coming, Tam?" Monica says, swinging around. Tammy, looking just as shocked as Ebony, scrambles to jam her lip-gloss and phone into her purse.

Ebony is already yapping into both of her cell phones before the bathroom door is even closed. "You won't believe what I just heard…"

"Look at this!" Shannon says, tossing a Victoria Secrets catalog in front of Erica. "This has got to be the cutest bra I have ever seen!" She continues, cramming the remainder of a rice cake in her mouth.

"You know," Jenna begins. "Just because they're rice cakes, doesn't mean they don't have calories. If you keep stuffing your mouth like that, you're going to start looking like Raven Symone before she lost all the weight."

Ashamed, Shannon chucks the rest of her rice cakes in a trash bin. She gazes out of the large window overlooking Jenna's freshly mowed front lawn. She looses herself in the warmth of the afternoon sun.

Jenna's plush room is packed with as many soft pillows of pink and plum hues as humanly possible. The faint scent of jasmine wafts through the air. The Dolls always find it easier to fend off 'the Mondays' with a relaxing afternoon at Jenna's.

"I was thinking," Erica starts. "The party is in just a few days. Maybe we should tell Lauren to come." Jenna cups her hand over her mouth. "I think I just threw up a little bit." Jenna rags. Shannon laughs a bit too hard. "Anyway," Erica continues. "It's not like you can just completely ban her from being a Doll."

Jenna takes a break from flipping through the reams of clothes hanging in her closet. Walking across the room, she plops down in front of Erica. "So you think I'm being too mean?" Jenna asks. "Yeah, a little." Erica replies timidly.

Before Jenna can continue her inquiry, each of the girl's jewel-encrusted cell phones begins to buzz – text messages. Scrambling to pick up their phones, the girls read silently.

Hey People!

I was hoping to see all of my sexy singles at The Dolls' Ball next Friday, but since most of you weren't invited anyway, I've decided to go to the REAL party this Friday...Tammy Olsen's! Not only is she fun and actually nice to people, but her party is going to be better anyway! Text ya later!

2hot4U

"Who in the world is 2hot4U?" Erica asks aloud. "And how did they get our personal cell numbers?"

"I bet it's Lauren texting us from a new number!" Shannon says.

"You're right." Jenna concludes. "Who else would have all of our numbers? Am I still being too mean?" She snaps.

"I'm calling Lauren right now!" Shannon roars. "Don't bother." Jenna replies. "She probably won't even answer. And why the heck would she send an email like that to us, anyway?"

"Maybe she didn't just send it to us." Erica says. "Maybe she sent it to everybody!"

"She wouldn't." Jenna says, not quite convinced.

"Well maybe she didn't." Shannon says. "Maybe she just sent it to us, like she's trying to get back at us or something for making her eat lunch alone."

"Not even." Erica says, reading another text on her phone. "I just got a text from Ebony. She says that the whole school is talking about three things: Tammy's party, the email about Jenna, and 2hot4U's text."

"I can't believe that Lauren would do something like this!" Shannon fumes.

"Wait a minute?" Jenna says, ceasing all other conversation. "What email about me?"

The Dolls huddle around Jenna's hot pink Apple iPad as she accesses her C. Edwards email account. Checking the inbox folder, she scans the emails until she comes across the most recent email. It's from another mysterious unknown sender. Jenna reads the email aloud.

Dear C. Edwards Middle School

This is your favorite Doll, just stopping by to give you an update on the biggest party of the year. Not only are we going to have the best music, but we're also having a special guest announcement. See you there – if you're invited.

Fast fact: Jenna wet her pants at a birthday party in the fourth grade.

Stay Tuned!

#1 Doll

Jenna's voice trails off as she reads the last line. The Dolls stare at the screen in absolute silence. Jenna is stunned. She doesn't know how to take this. She wants to cry. But she also wants to strangle someone.

"I ate dog food once." Erica announces. Jenna and Shannon look at her like she's crazy. "What?" Erica says. "I just thought I'd say something to lighten the mood." She places her hand on Jenna's shoulder. "I mean; that was a really brave thing for you to admit...to everyone...in the entire school."

"I didn't write that, you ditz!" Jenna yells. "Someone else sent that email and made me look like an idiot!"

Shannon shakes her head in disbelief. "Yeah, but who would do a thing like that?"

Monday afternoon at a high school isn't much different than Monday afternoon at a middle school. It's just more of the same. More kids, more afterschool clubs, more teachers and more attitudes.

And no one, especially no freshman brings more attitude than Constance Bowman – former Doll. A freshman cheerleader, Constance is just skirting out of the Brooksville High gymnasium at 4 o'clock when she is nearly blindsided by Monica.

"Excuse you!" Constance snarls.

"Sorry." Monica mumbles.

"Wait a tic." Constance says. "I know you. You're the YouTube slut from last year." She laughs.

"It's Monica." She responds coldly.

"Yeah, whatever. What are you doing here?" Constance asks. "I'm here to see you." Monica replies sheepishly. "Why would I want to see you?" Constance scoffs. "Because everyone is talking about what happened. Haven't you heard?"

"Heard what? Hurry up and spit it out!" Constance says, getting annoyed.

"Jenna Arnold has been saying that she is by far the best Doll to ever attend C. Edwards. She's running around school saying that you shouldn't have even been a Doll in the first place!"

Constance sucks her teeth. "The nerve of that ungrateful little brat!" She screams. Jenna is lucky we even let her become a Doll in the first place!

Constance doesn't waste any time telling Monica exactly how she feels about Jenna. She rips her former protégé, exposing the surprising truth in the process as Monica secretly captures it all on Lauren's phone. So much for the sisterhood of The Dolls.

Gossip runs rampant in most high schools, middle schools and even elementary schools for that matter. But this week, C. Edwards Middle School has seen the gossip fly off the Richter scale.

And for the first time this school year, Jenna isn't the one pulling the strings. She's one of the people being gossiped about and it's no surprise that she doesn't like it. Every kid, and even some teachers, can't stop giggling about the emails being sent from the mysterious "Unknown" email account. That's right, emails – as in more than one. Each day there's a new disgusting little tidbit about miss perfect, Jenna Arnold.

TUESDAY

Hey Party People,

The big bash is just three days away. And even though it's not related at all, I thought you should know that on her eleventh birthday Jenna's mother bought her prescription strength deodorant for her body odor!

#1 Doll,

WEDNESDAY

Hey All,

Two days left! Guess what? Jenna once got motion sickness while she was riding her bike and she threw up into the basket attached to the handlebars.

#1 Doll,

"This is the worst week of my life!" Jenna grumbles. Shannon and Erica sit on opposite sides of their friend on the Spirit Bench comparing charm bracelets. Shannon looks up just in time to spot a familiar face.

"It just might be getting worse." Shannon says as Lauren approaches. M.I.A. since their big blow up in the lunchroom, Lauren struts towards the girls with authority. Her heals kick up small clumps of grass as she crosses the school lawn.

"What do you want?" Jenna snarls. "Oh give it a rest, Mrs. Peabody!" Lauren roars back. Shannon and Erica do their best to muffle their giggles. "I've read the emails." Lauren says. "Looks like the queen got knocked off her throne." She smiles.

"Well you should know." Jenna says. "You're the one who wrote the emails in the first place!"

Lauren seems insulted. "Not even! I've got better things to do than waste my time making fun of you." She says.

"Oh don't act so innocent." Replies Jenna. "You sent those emails just like you wrote that stupid text message. Just admit it."

Lauren takes off her gold-rimmed D&G shades and tucks them in the matching tote. Taking her time she addresses Jenna. "First of all," Lauren says. "I lost my cell phone last week, so I couldn't have sent any text message! And…"

"Hold on!" Erica interrupts, waiving her pink-tipped index finger from side to side. "If you really didn't send the text message," she says, pointing at Lauren. "Then someone else is really out to get us!"

The Dolls stare at each other mulling over the revelation. They just can't fathom that someone would actually want to embarrass them. They're the freaking Dolls for crying out loud. They are C. Edwards Middle School royalty. Who would want to embarrass them?

Before anyone can answer that question, Shannon's phone begins vibrating incessantly. "Another text, from me I suppose." Lauren says snidely. "Actually," Shannon says, ignoring Lauren's tone of voice. "I set my phone to receive any email sent to my school account just in case someone sent an email talking bad about me…or one of you guys, of course." She clarifies, looking around at the other Dolls.

THURSDAY

Hey Lovers,

The Doll's Ball is practically here. So get ready…except for everyone who isn't invited. LOL. All of you should just go to Tammy's big bash. It's gonna be great!

BTW – In fifth grade, Jenna ate fish eggs and loved it!

#1 Doll,

Shannon stops reading aloud but she keeps staring at her phone, partly so that she doesn't have to face Jenna and partly so that she can re-read the last sentence about the fish eggs. Gross!

"It was caviar!" Jenna explodes. "It's a delicacy. People eat caviar all the time!" Jenna snatches Shannon's phone from her grasp and reads the email for herself. Seething with anger, she hands the phone back to Shannon who is still too afraid to make eye contact.

Erica frantically searches her purse for a piece of gum. She unwraps a piece of Orbitz and pops it in her mouth, chewing nervously. "Want some?" She says, offering some gum first to Shannon and then Lauren. "No thanks. I'm not a Doll, remember?" Lauren says.

"Oh get over yourself!" Jenna shouts. "Of course you're a Doll. Besides, we've got bigger problems than you. Our party is tomorrow and on top of that, little miss perfect is having a party on the same night!"

Jenna grabs her purse from its resting place on the Spirit Bench and riffles through it until she locates her Berry Cherry lip-gloss. She erratically applies the gloss to her lips as she exhales deeply trying to calm her nerves.

"Maybe it's Tammy." Lauren suggests. I mean, you said it yourself. She's throwing a party on the same night. Who else would know all of that stuff about you?"

That's when Jenna realizes that Lauren is partially right. There are only two people who would know about the peeing incident and the caviar. But there is only one person who would dare say anything about it. *Monica Jackson!*

"You look great honey." Mrs. Jackson remarks as she watches Monica brushing her hair. Mrs. Jackson takes a seat on Monica's bed. She's unable to take her eyes off her daughter. "Why don't you try wearing your hair up?" She suggests. Monica, standing in front of her vanity, now fastening her earrings, rolls her eyes at her mother. "Mom, please."

"Sorry." Mrs. Jackson says, rolling her eyes right back at Monica. "I just think that you have such a pretty face and neck. Why hide it behind all of that hair? Besides, if you wear it down, you look older and the boys at the party may be too intimidated to talk you."

"Good!" Shouts Mr. Jackson as he walks by the open door.

Monica grabs a handful of her hair and pulls it back into a ponytail. Maybe mom is right. She wonders. But then again, older is always better and moms are rarely right. So she lets her hair fall back to her shoulders.

"Is Johnny going to Tammy's party?" Mrs. Jackson asks, changing the subject.

"I don't think he'll be there." Monica answers. He probably has other plans." She smacks her lips and smiles at her reflection. "OK, mom. I think I'm ready." She says, checking her jeans for any wrinkles.

"Call us when you're ready to be picked up from Tammy's." Mrs. Jackson shouts as Monica strolls down the driveway. "I don't want you walking home in the dark."

"OK, mom. I will." Monica says, shooing her mom back inside the house, more than waving at her.

Monica hurries down Peachtree Street until she makes a right on Trinity. But instead of taking the next left on to Clermont, Monica bypasses Tammy's block and walks three blocks further down Trinity Street...to Jenna's house.

Still a few houses away from Jenna's, Monica is surprised to see a large crowd of kids gathered in Jenna's front lawn. It's practically a who's who of C. Edwards Middle School. Each of the VIPs clutches his or her Golden Ticket as they wait around the Arnold's front yard. Some kids are growing impatient and check the clock on their cell phones every few seconds.

Jenna's home is one of the larger houses in the development. When they were younger, Monica, Tammy and Jenna would spend hours running around the house playing hide-n-seek. On occasion Jenna's dad would let the girls hang out in his "man cave" where the pool table and Sharper Image massage chair seemed to beg them to come play.

It's been months since Monica stood in this yard, not to mention inside the house. She keeps her head tilted down and tries to nonchalantly join the growing crowd on Jenna's front lawn. Suddenly, the front door to Jenna's house opens.

Mrs. Arnold, a former JC Penny's catalogue model, steps onto the porch. Her light brown hair is full of body and it sweeps from side to side each time she looks in a new direction. She smiles at the children with a regal, yet distant look in her eyes.

"Quite please." Mrs. Arnold says. "I know you've been waiting to come inside. Well I just received word that the guests of honor are about to arrive."

Right on cue, a black hummer limousine approaches the house. The Dolls cram themselves through the sunroof and wave to their loyal subjects. The crowd immediately erupts; kids start screaming as if The Dolls are celebrities.

The hummer comes to a halt in front of Jenna's home. A chauffer hops out of the driver's seat and scoots around to the passenger door.

"May I introduce," he bellows in a baritone voice. "Jenna, Lauren, Erica and Shannon!" The crowd goes wild again as he jacks the door open, practically ripping it off the hinges.

Even their driver is dramatic. Monica muses.

Each of The Dolls takes her time stepping out of the car, soaking up the cheers from the admirers and wannabes and posing for the photographers from the school paper.

First Shannon, then Erica and then Lauren; one by one they address the fans, waving like princesses and posturing seductively. The Dolls strut up the walkway to the house where Mrs. Arnold snaps pictures on her digital camera.

But where's Jenna? This is her house after all. The guests begin buzzing with anticipation. "I thought I saw her in the limo." Whispers a girl as she tries in vain to peer through the hummer's tinted windows.

The buzz settles to a barely audible undertone of voices. Without warning, the sound of trumpets begins to blare from a pair of speakers that rest against the garage door.

At last Jenna steps out of the hummer, looking every bit a queen. She dawns a strapless platinum cocktail dress that is much too adult for a thirteen year-old. Her hair is pulled to the side and flows just over the edge of her left collarbone. The cheering consumes the air.

Things aren't quite as theatrical a few blocks away at the party Monica *should* be attending. But it's no less impressive. Tammy stands behind the island in the kitchen with her mother frantically pouring Tropical Fruit Kool-Aid. The house is packed with kids! It seems like every two minutes another group of middle school kids ring the doorbell.

"Who are all these kids?" Tammy's mother asks, as she grabs another bag of plastic cups. Mrs. Olsen is auditioning for the role of homemaker. Until recently, she worked for the largest advertising firm in the area. But after the company downsized, letting her go in the process, Mrs. Olsen decided it was time to try the whole stay at home mom "thing."

"I don't know." Tammy answers. Ice rings down into a cup from the icemaker in the door of the refrigerator. "I guess I know some of them, but the rest of them just look like familiar faces."

Indeed, the growing crowd at Tammy's house is compiled of "everyone else" in the school who wasn't invited to The Dolls' Ball. Geeks, nerds, Goths, and all of the run-of-the-mill average kids from C. Edwards fill up every single room of the first floor of Tammy's house.

"I'm gonna grab my Ipod and turn on some music." Tammy announces, slipping out of the kitchen. "Tam!" Her mother shouts after her. "What am I suppose to do with…" It's too late, Tammy's sliding her way through the crowd and Mrs. Olsen loses sight of her in a sea of kids.

Darting between partygoers, Tammy runs right past Johnny, who is lounging on the plush couch in the center of the living room. "Hey Tammy!" He says jumping to his feet. He stretches for her arm but Tammy is just out of reach as she splits a pair of eighth-graders. "Have you seen Monica?" He yells after her. But he has about as much luck getting Tammy's attention as Mrs. Olsen.

Safely in her bedroom, Tammy snatches her cell phone from her dresser. Scanning her recent calls she selects Monica's first grade headshot and waits impatiently for her best friend to pick up.

"Hello?" Monica whispers.

"Monica!" Tammy says. "Where in the world are you? And why are you talking so quietly?"

Monica slinks away from the crowd of kids that begin to gather around the Arnold's front door. The Dolls continue to smile and pose for the kids while an old Katy Perry song plays over the speakers.

"It's a long story." Monica answers, trying to avoid further discussion about her whereabouts. But the raucous crowd still gathered outside of Jenna's house, foils any thoughts of secrecy.

"What the heck is all that noise?" Asks Tammy as she pulls her ear away from the receiver. "Nothing, nothing," Monica lies, whispering even lower.

"You're at Jenna's!" Tammy yells when the little light bulb in her head finally flashes. "I can't believe this!" Tammy explodes. Flustered, she starts pacing her room, thoughts of the increasingly large party downstairs bubbling in her mind.

"Tam, just calm down." Monica says trying to reason with her.

"I don't need to calm down!" Tammy shouts. "You are the reason I'm having this party in the first place. I didn't even want to do it. Now I've got half of the school downstairs and you skip our party to go see Jenna!"

"Tammy you don't understand. I'm here to make sure The Dolls get what they deserve." Monica explains. "Oh." Says Tammy. "So I guess I was just pawn in your plan to get revenge on Jenna."

Tired of Monica's excuses, Tammy not only hangs up, she turns her phone off as well. She hurls her cell on the bed and stares at her reflection in the large oak vintage mirror hanging above her dresser. Tammy runs her right hand through her long flowing mane. She frowns a bit, noticing that her Old Navy Tee isn't concealing her "friends" as much as she thought it would. As she contemplates changing shirts, she hears a knock at the door.

"Tammy?" Her mother calls out. "Are you coming back downstairs?"

"Just a minute, mom."

"Ok, honey. But hurry. Everyone is asking for you."

"They're asking for me?" Tammy questions.

"Of course." Mrs. Olsen replies. "It's your party, silly."

There goes that light bulb in the brain again. It begins to occur to Tammy that all of those kids down there came to *her* party. They may not be jocks and cheerleaders and rich kids. But neither is she.

Looking back at the pretty girl in the mirror, Tammy smiles. She still feels like she stole Nicki Minaj's breasts. And she still feels awkward in all but three of her outfits. But for the first time in a long time, Tammy feels comfortable in her own skin.

Monica groans while watching the kids in front of Jenna's house. She can't believe that they are still fawning over The Dolls even after all of the emails that #1 Doll aka Monica, sent this week.

"Everyone listen up." Jenna announces over a bullhorn. Please have your tickets ready as you make your way into the house.

The crowd of kids begins to funnel through the front door of Jenna's home.

Monica takes a deep breath before blending into the mass. Just when it seems like she's actually going to slip inside, Monica hears a familiar shrill voice echoing in her direction.

"What are you doing here?" Jenna says, pushing against the grain of the crowd as she makes her way over to Monica.

A cold chill trickles down Monica's back as Jenna confronts her. "You must be even dumber than you look, MJ." Says Jenna. The kids begin to take notice and everyone stops moving through the large foyer.

"First, you send those emails about me and now you think you'll get into my party?" Jenna growls. "Not even!" She says, answering her own question.

Uninterested in being berated by Jenna, Monica turns and begins pushing her way back out of the house.

"MJ, you are a loser!" Jenna shouts as Monica nears the door. "You think people like you but they don't!"

Monica turns around and smiles. "Join the club, Jenna. Join the club." She says before exiting.

A short kid with shaggy hair and baggy pants eases the door shut after Monica leaves. But Monica has come too far not to witness her triumph. As soon as the door closes, Monica scoots around to the side of the house and peeks into a window looking into the Arnold's large living room.

The kids pile into the Arnold family living room. "We're really sorry that we couldn't get a big band to come play for you guys tonight," Jenna says, glaring at Lauren. "But it's not a total loss. Lauren's mom booked the best belly dancers in town to entertain us tonight."

Outside the Arnold's home, Monica holds up Lauren's phone and pushes send. A wave of cell phone ringtones washes throughout the party. One by one, the kids open the video message sent directly from Lauren's phone.

It's Constance Bowman, the one girl who still has more clout at C. Edwards than Jenna.

"You must be joking." Constance says as the video clip begins playing. "Jenna Arnold is a nobody." Constance continues. The kids in the room gasp in unison. "Jenna wouldn't even be a Doll if it wasn't for the whole YouTube slut incident. Jenna is a replacement, a scab. She's a wannabe that happened to get lucky! We picked her and those other girls because we had to pick someone. But this year's Dolls are pathetic."

A chorus of jeers rustles through the crowd as the kids watch the video on their phones. Jenna, who watches in horror on her own cell phone, clears her throat preparing to dismiss Constance's ravings as a jealous rant aimed at girls far superior in everyway. But she doesn't. Jenna looks at all of the faces. The silent audience comprised of all of her peers waits for her to address them. They wait for her scathing response. But she doesn't give one. Jenna lowers her chin and begins to cry, softly at first but it builds into a flood of irrepressible tears.

"Everybody get out!" Jenna screams in between her sobbing. She shoves her way through the crowd and sprints up the winding staircase to the second floor.

The kids look around at each other for answers. After a wide display of uncertain expressions, one voice, lost in the sea of shrugging shoulders says, "That's what she gets for being so mean all the time!" Soon, kids begin to shake their heads in agreement as they chuckle to themselves.

The kids file out of the party and there is almost a sense of relief that Jenna has been officially knocked from her pedestal. The witch is dead!

At last, Jenna is the one that is embarrassed and she can feel what it is like to have someone you trust make you look like a fool in front of everyone. This is the moment Monica has dreamt about. So why isn't she happy?

Near tears herself, Monica steps away from the window and leaves Jenna's for good.

"Go Tammy! Go Tammy!" The excited chant springs from inside Tammy's home as Monica strolls up the driveway. Kids mull around the interior of the open front door.

"Where did all these kids come from?" Monica wonders aloud. "Most of them have been here all evening." A familiar voice hollers. "But the rest of them just got here." Monica whirls around to find Johnny leaning against a closet door. "Johnny?" Monica says curiously. "I thought you'd be at Jenna's party."

Johnny pushes himself off of the closet door and hands Monica a flash drive. "Nope. I've been waiting for you. Just like I have been all week."

Ouch.

"Look, I know I haven't been a good class partner, but I've been kind of busy." Monica says, batting her eyelashes, hoping to appeal to Johnny's soft side. But he just shakes his head in disappointment. "Blowing me off so that you can do whatever is one thing. But I didn't think you'd miss out on your best friend's party."

"You don't understand." Monica argues. "I was at Jenna's. I was making sure that she got what she deserved!"

"Well I hope it was worth it." Johnny sighs. "This flash drive has all of my research on our class topic. Maybe you can take a look when you're not busy blowing off your friends."

Not wanting to give Monica the satisfaction of making up an excuse, Johnny forces his way through the crowd to the corner of the living room where Chunk holds court, entertaining a group of rowdy football players.

Monica rushes out of Tammy's house at a time when kids are trickling in from The Dolls' Ball. Instead of heading for home, she heads straight to Tammy's backyard for a few moments of peace and quite.

When Monica, Jenna and Tammy were in elementary school, their favorite hangout spot was the large wooden playhouse that Mr. Olsen built when the girls were in first grade. The girls would spend hours having picnics and tea parties in the privacy of their very own "house."

Monica stops in front of the playhouse and studies the old hangout. She studies the faded green paint and worn plywood. It's smaller than I remember. She thinks.

She ducks her head and crouches inside. Monica takes two half steps and sits down, resting her head against the wall of the house that Jenna once dubbed, the west wing.

Alone with her thoughts, Monica closes her eyes and wonders how she could possibly make such a mess of things. Not only are Johnny and Tammy upset with her, but she also feels horrible that she embarrassed Jenna.

As the evening sets in, the temperature cools a bit. Monica listens to the sounds of her classmates enjoying themselves inside Tammy's party – which has turned out to be the best party in school history. The rumbling bass of hip-hop music nearly rocks Monica to sleep as she sits on the floor in the playhouse.

"I thought I'd find you here." Tammy says, startling Monica. "I heard you were at the party but I looked around the house I couldn't find you. That's when I thought about this spot."

Tammy bends down and takes a seat on the floor, careful not to get any grass stains on her clothes from the weeds that have grown between the cracks in the wood.

"How was The Dolls' Ball?" She asks. "I guess it went well." Monica mumbles. "Jenna was so embarrassed that she started crying." Tammy forces a smile. "That's good...right?"

"That's the thing." Monica blurts out in frustration. "You'd think I'd be happy that Jenna got what she deserved. But I'm not. I feel worse than ever." She wipes a single tear from the corner of her eye.

"Since the end of last school year I wanted to make Jenna pay for what she did to me. She embarrassed me in front of the whole school. But today, when I saw her crying and all of the kids were laughing at her; all I could think about was how bad I felt when I was in her position."

"Don't worry about it. What's done is done." Tammy says scooting towards Monica. "Besides, sitting around pouting while people are partying is not going to help."

"Tam, I'm sorry." Monica whispers. "I mean it. I really screwed things up. You're the last person I'd want to hurt. I just got so caught up in this plan to get revenge. But in the end, I guess I'm no better than Jenna." Tammy puts her arm around her sulking best friend. "Trust me." Tammy says. "You're a much better friend that she ever was."

"Really?"

"Of course!" Tammy says. "Not only are you a better friend than Jenna, but you've also got one of the cutest boys in school as your class partner."

"Oh no." Groans Monica. "I forgot all about Johnny. He hates me right now. And I can't blame him. I haven't been much of a partner."

"Chill out, Mon. I'm sure you two can catch up on your schoolwork." Tammy consoles her.

Monica rolls over on all fours and crawls out of the playhouse. She turns to help Tammy escape from the tight quarters. "Guess we're not five years old anymore, huh?" Tammy jokes as she checks her clothes for stains.

Monica smirks at the thought. She dusts herself off and complains. "The entire school year, I've wanted to tell Johnny how much I like him."

"Um, Monica?" Tammy tries to interrupt. "To tell him how cute he looks." Monica continues, ignoring Tammy. "Every time he yawns near the end of class, I just want him to wrap those strong arms around me."

"Monica!"

"Every time he smiles, I just want to kiss those soft lips and…"

"Monica, shut up!"

"What! What is it?" Monica exclaims. Tammy delicately puts her hands on Monica's shoulders and swings her around. "It's Johnny." Tammy says. Monica's heart sinks from her chest. So freaking embarrassing!

"Um, hi Monica." Johnny says.

"Hi." She replies, looking into Johnny's never-ending eyes. "So exactly how much of that did you hear?" She asks.

"Oh, I didn't really hear anything. Just the part about my arms and my kissable lips, but nothing else."

"Great." Monica says snidely. "Hey Tam, can you please give us a minute?"

"Sure. I need to check on my guests anyway." Tammy sweeps past the lovebirds as she makes her way inside the house.

"Johnny here's the thing." Monica says. "I like you. I mean I really like you. That night at my house, I wanted us to kiss. And I know I'm not as popular as The Dolls. And I don't have all the new clothes that they do. And I don't eat sushi or go on exotic trips. But I like myself just the way I am. So if you can't look past all of the glitz and glam of The Dolls, then it's your loss."

"You're right."

"Huh?" Monica replies. "I said you're right." Johnny repeats himself. "*Anybody* who looks just at the surface is going to miss out on a lot of great things in life. But the truth is that I like you. I've wanted to go out with you since Mr. B made us partners." Shocked, Monica asks, "Well why didn't you say something?"

"I didn't know how. I wanted to, but then I punked out." Johnny confesses.

"I wish I knew that you had a thing for me." Monica says softly. Johnny takes her tenderly by the hand. Monica hangs her head low. But Johnny brushes her face upward with a gentle gesture. "Don't worry about it." He says. "I can't help it." She replies. "I'm so embarrassed."

"Monica." Johnny tries to interrupt.

"First I don't even realize that you like me." Monica continues.

"Monica!" Johnny tries again.

"Then I completely ignore you while I plot on Jenna." Monica keeps rambling.

"Hello?"

"And after all of that, I didn't even enjoy watching her squirm."

"Monica?"

"What?" She yells.

Without warning Johnny pulls Monica closely by the waist, leans forward, and kisses her. It's a little awkward yet amazingly beautiful. The kiss lasts only for a few seconds but it is one that Monica will remember for the rest of her life.

As their lips part, Monica stands frozen, her eyes closed and her mouth slightly open. Seconds float past when at last her eyes flutter open. She gazes at Johnny.

In the world of teenagers, nothing lasts forever. But as they stand in the evening shade of Tammy's house among the manicured bushes planted flush against the side of the home; Monica and Johnny try to hold onto this pure moment.

OLSEN'S FRONT YARD – SAME NIGHT

An increasingly loud murmuring begins to bubble into a full-blown argument that can't be ignored. Giving into the annoyance and curiosity; the couple dashes around the houses to the front door.

"Excuse me?" Lauren scoffs. "You can't do this to us. We're The Dolls!" She protests. Dozens of kids stand behind in between The Dolls and Tammy's front door. Some of the kids stuff their heads out of the windows to get a glimpse of The Dolls, who – for the first time ever – stand on the outside looking in.

"Nobody wants you here!" One girl shouts, as cheers of support erupt from within the house. "Look around." Another kid yells, gesturing inside the house and stretching his arm towards the front lawn and driveway where kids stand, watching the scene unfold.

"These are all of the kids that weren't invited to your perfect people party." An eighth grader chimes in. "These are all of the kids that you said aren't good enough."

Jenna, Lauren, Shannon and Erica scan the premises. Erica looks ashamed. Shannon seems embarrassed. Jenna and Lauren? They're angry. "Just shut up!" Jenna hisses. "This party won't be worth crap unless we're here! Besides, this isn't even your house, you freak. Where's Tammy anyway."

Within a few seconds, Tammy emerges from the house. She stands in the doorway looking like a reluctant queen. A towering street lamp cascading over the neighborhood begins to flicker on, casting a soft glow on Tammy's glimmering frock.

All eyes, including Monica's, focus on Tammy as the whispers flowing throughout the crowd come to a halt.

"Hi Jenna." Tammy says.

"God, Tammy." Lauren exclaims. "It's about time you came out here." Tammy ignores Lauren, focusing only on Jenna. "Jenna, a year ago, we were best friends."

"Yeah, what a difference a year makes." Lauren snickers. "And then one day." Tammy continues, still ignoring Lauren. "You just dumped us. And for what...them?"

Jenna rolls her eyes. "Tam, you just don't get it. I'm a Doll. I have to be friends with other Dolls and you just weren't..."

"Good enough?" Tammy says, cutting her off. "Because that's how I felt. Like I wasn't good enough. I felt like I wasn't cool enough, funny enough and most of all, I felt like I wasn't pretty enough. I spent the whole summer wishing I was more like you. But I finally realize that I'm fine being me. I don't have to push people around or start rumors about people just because they're different or because we may not see eye to eye. So if you want to come to our party, I'm cool with that. You're friends," She says using air quotes, "can come too. But leave the attitude on the doorstep, because everyone here deserves to be treated with respect."

Monica smiles broadly. Chills run down her spine as she watches her best friend grow up right before her eyes. Jenna once again, scans the crowd. Her eyes are glossed with impending tears. At a loss for words, she takes a deep breath, clinches her jaw and stifles her tears.

"That's right, go ahead and cry, you little baby!" Screams someone in the crowd.

The kids, most of whom were not invited to The Dolls' Ball in the first place, begin to whisper and giggle at the mere thought of Queen Jenna, breaking down in tears. Jenna and The Dolls begin to shrink under the weight of taunting coming from all directions. Jenna's facial expressions dance between furious and helpless.

"That's enough!" Monica commands.

Monica lets Johnny's hand slip from her grasp and she walks across the lawn to front porch where The Dolls still stand at Tammy's doorstep. "I've waited for a moment like this since last school year." Monica says. "I wanted to embarrass Jenna. I wanted her to cry like she made me cry." Jenna looks away, too ashamed to face Monica.

"You know what?" Monica looks directly at Jenna. "She deserves it. But if there's one thing I've learned today, it's that putting her in that position makes me no better than them." She gestures towards The Dolls. And I don't want to be like that. I want to be better than that. I'm finished worrying about my ex-best friends."

Monica walks up to Tammy and puts her arm around her. "Now I'm focusing on being a better person and being there for my real best friends."

END

www.ingramcontent.com/pod-product-compliance
Lightning Source LLC
Chambersburg PA
CBHW070922130626
46555CB00001B/242